ANYTHING GOES

180 40 1203

27/11 3

Also available from Headline Liaison

Temptation by Cathryn Cooper
Seduction by Cathryn Cooper
Change Partners by Cathryn Cooper
Obsession by Cathryn Cooper
Green Silk by Cathryn Cooper
Act of Exposure by Cathryn Cooper
The Journal by James Allen
Love Letters by James Allen
The Diary by James Allen
Out of Control by Rebecca Ambrose
Aphrodisia by Rebecca Ambrose
A Private Affair by Carol Anderson
Voluptuous Voyage by Lacey Carlyle
Magnolia Moon by Lacey Carlyle
Vermilion Gates by Lucinda Chester
The Challenge by Lucinda Chester
The Paradise Garden by Aurelia Clifford
Hearts on Fire by Tom Crewe and Amber Wells
Sleepless Nights by Tom Crewe and Amber Wells
Dangerous Desires by J J Duke
Seven Days by J J Duke
A Scent of Danger by Sarah Hope-Walker
Private Lessons by Cheryl Mildenhall
Intimate Strangers by Cheryl Mildenhall
Dance of Desire by Cheryl Mildenhall

Anything Goes

Cathryn Cooper

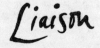

Copyright © 1998 Cathryn Cooper

The right of Cathryn Cooper to be identified as the Author of
the Work has been asserted by her in accordance with the
Copyright, Designs and Patents Act 1988.

First published in 1998
by HEADLINE BOOK PUBLISHING

A HEADLINE LIAISON paperback

10 9 8 7 6 5 4 3 2 1

All rights reserved. No part of this publication may be
reproduced, stored in a retrieval system, or transmitted,
in any form or by any means without the prior written
permission of the publisher, nor be otherwise circulated
in any form of binding or cover other than that in which
it is published and without a similar condition being
imposed on the subsequent purchaser.

All characters in this publication are fictitious
and any resemblance to real persons, living or dead,
is purely coincidental.

ISBN 0 7472 5819 8

Typeset by
Letterpart Limited, Reigate, Surrey

Printed and bound in Great Britain by
Mackays of Chatham plc, Chatham, Kent

HEADLINE BOOK PUBLISHING
A division of Hodder Headline PLC
338 Euston Road
London NW1 3BH

Anything Goes

Prologue

The Catnip Club is no more, sad to say. There's a restaurant there now with a pretty courtyard and a band that plays modern jazz to foreign tourists.

Sophistication, coupled with decadent debauchery, might seem to be modern words invented by the faster, sexually hedonistic people of the late twentieth century. But these people drinking mint julep and ordering deep-fried chicken are fooling themselves. Although their eyes and cameras capture what they can of the old Latin Quarter of New Orleans, they cannot recreate the full flavour of what it used to be.

Only if you dip deep into your imagination and block out the sound of synthetic jazz do you catch the last echoes of another time.

Back in the twenties, the Catnip Club was a place of blue smoke, sensuality you could taste, and throbbing music that was so raw you could almost cut it with a saw-edged knife.

The rule was 'anything goes'. And anything did. These are the stories of those who tasted life and love, both the decadent and the sophisticated.

Chapter 1

It was a warm March day in 1925 when Shirley Anne Potter packed her best underwear and two decent outfits in a well-worn carpet bag that might have been brought to Louisiana by some white, Yankee ancestor.

Family history was the last thing on her mind on that warm day when the cotton buds were sprouting and powder-puff clouds were already skidding across the dawn sky. Her present life was what really mattered. Her mind was made up, but leaving wasn't easy.

Errol was still sleeping, his curly hair shining blue-black against the pillow.

I'm sure going to miss him, Shirley Anne thought sadly, her eyes raking the lean brown form slumbering naked on the bed. His skin gleamed with a patina of sweat due partly to the high humidity so prevalent in Louisiana, and partly as a result of what they had done together just a few hours ago.

'My, but you're one helluva lover,' she whispered. She hugged herself in an effort to recapture the feel of his limbs entwined with hers, the hardness of his chest and his groin as he'd pinned her to the bed.

Swallowing a heartfelt sigh, she studied him, determined

to memorise every glistening muscle, every curve, every indent of his body.

Black lashes fluttered in response to some secret dream he was having. There was a certain pinkness beneath the dark skin of his cheeks, a moist shininess on his upper lip.

She breathed in his scent, the smell of his body tempting her own. The urge to go back to bed and curve the front of her body against the back of his was incredibly strong. It was a mighty temptation. Yet if she was to seek fame and fortune in New Orleans, she had to leave him like this, in secret.

Confrontation had always been something she tried to avoid. Not that angry words would have lasted long. They would soon have been replaced by a kiss, then a caress. In no time at all, her body would have fallen slave to her own sexuality. She knew he would have persuaded her to stay. It would have been so easy.

No, she insisted. *Look at him while you can. Remember him exactly as he is now.*

His flesh was firm and devoid of body hair except for the nest of crinkled blackness between his thighs. From amid the hair, his penis lay; soft now and curled to one side, sleeping like the rest of his body.

Like a snake, she thought to herself with a smile. Like a dark brown, one-eyed snake, layered in upon itself. Without form. Without life.

When she was with him, though, it woke up; became a thing of power, of rippling muscle and thumping blood.

Last night, in the midst of fervent passion, he'd said he loved her. She'd believed him, yet, even as his hands had caressed her breasts and played fast and loose with her nipples, she had only moaned her delight. Not once had she told him about leaving for New Orleans; about seeing a world other than that surrounding the deep, dark bayous of Southern Louisiana.

Thinking of his hands on her breasts made her shudder. For a moment her resolve left her. She reached out to touch the dark waves that feathered over the nape of his neck. But her other need, the one to be somebody, to taste the excitement of the outside world, was too strong.

'Hell,' she whispered to herself. 'Do you want to be buried here forever? Your skin's peachy soft right now, but what about when it's as cracked as some old apple left at the bottom of the barrel?'

The analogy wasn't lost on her. Memories, she thought, would be the only salve to soothe those crinkled lines, and she had a strong yearning for some real hot memories to savour in her old age. New Orleans it had to be.

She pulled her hand back, bent down and picked up her bag. In the other she carried her best shoes that were black patent and very strappy. She must make no noise.

'Goodbye,' she said softly, turning one more time to gaze on the man she had known and loved all her life.

She didn't cry until she got to the bus stop, and she didn't realise she was still going barefoot until she tried to pay the driver and her shoes got in the way.

Chapter 2

Jungle rhythms screamed and pounded from beneath Shirley Anne's feet as the blues band in the club below belted out their first number. The vibrations shuddered across the floor, crept up her calves and made her thighs and her buttocks tremble. Even the delicate fabric of her underwear shivered against her flesh. She was aware that her breasts were quivering like two jellies just turned out from their moulds, but she was none too concerned about that.

The man who owned the club was walking around her, circles getting smaller as he got closer, and his scent getting stronger.

She liked his scent. Liked him too. Couldn't help holding her shoulders back so that her nipples pressed against the thin fabric of her dress. Couldn't help arching her spine so that the seams strained against the opulent voluptuousness of her buttocks.

Half hidden behind dark lashes, her eyes followed his progress. There was a certain arrogance to the way he held himself. His chin was high. His eyes regarded her from either side of an aquiline nose that ended in flaring nostrils.

He moved gracefully, and yet she detected something else beneath the suave, sophisticated surface. Something more vigorous. Something deeply decadent.

He was a handsome man, this Rene Brabonne who owned the Catnip Club. He was dark and sleek in his well-made clothes. He had the air of someone sure of his position, sure of his roots.

Because he wore no jacket, she could discern the shape of his arms beneath his cotton shirt. His bright mustard vest wrestled with the muscles of his chest. Its silk back gleamed with the effort of containing the understated muscularity of his body. He was lithe rather than broad.

She trembled with anticipation as he came to a standstill in front of her and a mix of maleness, cologne and other silk seemed to envelope her.

At first, her heart quaked at his closeness. A kind of fear made her direct her gaze at the floor which still trembled with the music from the club below.

But why was she doing this? It was as if she was not permitted to look at him. He could only look at her.

A well of sudden defiance rose within her. *I'm his equal*, she thought. Holding herself that much more erect, she tilted her chin, turned her head. Boldly, her dark green eyes looked into his.

He smiled; almost as if he understood why she was looking at him that way. His eyes twinkled. Like stars, she thought, stars fashioned from steel.

'What is your name, *chérie*?' His voice was deep, warm and tinged with the lilt of Louisiana Cajun that sounded as if it was struggling to be Parisienne French.

'Shirley Anne Potter, sir.'

'So what are you doing in New Orleans?'

The chill grey eyes of Rene Brabonne seemed never once to leave Shirley Anne's face, and yet her body trembled with the sure knowledge he had scrutinised the darkness of her hair, the creaminess of her skin, and the odd green lustre of her eyes.

Chin held high, she met his gaze.

'I needed a different life. I decided to come to New Orleans to get it.'

He nodded slowly. At the same time he blew a puff of smoke, then immediately slipped the cigar he was smoking between his teeth, chewing it as he moved away from her and sat himself down in a big leather chair behind an equally large cedar desk. He narrowed his eyes, and for a moment Shirley Anne was sure she could read his thoughts. There was lust there alongside something else she found difficult to understand.

He took the cigar from his mouth. 'Your looks could be your fortune, Shirley Anne, but that is not enough for the patrons of the Catnip Club. And it is not enough for me. There are too many delightful young women who rely on their bodies alone to make their fortune for them. I want more than that, so, if your voice matches your looks, I can take you on. Can you sing?'

A flock of nervous butterflies seemed to take flight in Shirley Anne's stomach. Sing? Of course she could sing. She nodded.

'Yes. I used to sing in Church. In the choir. Sometimes solo.'

Rene chuckled. 'We do not indulge in too much church music here, *chérie*, though some feel their sins are so great, they have a need to attend confession now and again. We do have a chorus of singing dancers. But I discern that you might be more than that. Am I right, Shirley Anne?'

A look of panic crossed Shirley Anne's face. Would the smooth voice that had charmed a church congregation charm the more sophisticated clientele of the Catnip Club? What would she do if he didn't like it?

Rene, seeing her anguished expression, got up from his chair and came to stand beside her. Without him touching her, she could feel the warmth of his body. Yet at the same time she wanted to feel him more closely.

'Do not be nervous, *chérie*. What else can you sing?'

Days roaming through swamp grass and drifting on water passed through Shirley Anne's mind. At the same time, so did a song, a deep, resonant song that Errol had written himself and taught only to her. Her voice rang out, full of emotion, full of soul, and strangely suiting the tempo of the band that played in the club downstairs.

> 'My, my, my green-eyed womannnn,
> Where, where, where have you been.
> You left me sittin' lonely here,
> Cheatin' girl, you bin seen . . .'

Barely a verse had escaped from her throat before Rene's hand was resting on her ribcage. She started, her voice breaking a little. But she saw Rene was smiling at her, his eyes twinkling, his darkly oiled moustache seeming to smile along with his mouth. She understood his intentions. He was feeling for the source of her song, assessing the way she breathed as it burst from her throat.

When the song came to an end, he hooked a thumb in the fob pocket of the pale mustard vest he was wearing. It was old but made of good stuff. Shirley Anne knew decent quality when she saw it.

'Your voice is as astonishing as your looks. It comes from deep inside. I can feel its strength – here.' He patted then pressed the concave area beneath her ribs.

Shirley Anne willed her empty stomach not to rumble.

She breathed more easily when Rene's free hand caressed her cheek. 'Creole. Mulatto,' he said, his voice suddenly dreamy. 'A mix of classical European and a hint of darkest, wildest Africa. Intoxicating.'

She looked into his eyes. What was it she could see there? Was she really as gifted with the second sight as her mother had said she was. Perhaps, but only when someone looked at her in a certain way could she really see what was in a man's thoughts. Like now. With Rene Brabonne. The image she saw in his mind frightened her. She could see her naked body stretched out, arms high above her head, chained to a wall, a whip reddening her flesh. She could almost feel his teeth upon her breasts and the thrust of his pelvis grinding against hers. She flushed at the thought of it.

Rene laughed, misinterpreting the reason for her sudden show of bashfulness.

'Please, don't be embarrassed. I am merely expressing my admiration for such a uniquely beautiful young woman. You're not frightened of me are you?' he asked.

Shirley Anne hesitated before answering. *I need him*, she thought. But at the same time she warned herself to be careful.

'No,' she whispered.

Again he placed his hand upon her ribcage. She did not protest. Her stomach muscles merely tensed as she waited for him to say the right words, the ones she wanted to hear.

'You will do me very well. I can even offer you accommodation. I own a house on St Pierre Boulevard. There is an upstairs apartment available there. I am sure you will be very comfortable.'

'I've got the job?'

She almost screeched the words. At the same time, the music from the club below reached a startling crescendo. Horn, sax and trombone collided in ear-splitting harmony. They sounded as if they were celebrating – like her.

Shirley Anne Potter was very pleased with herself. Two weeks had passed since arriving in New Orleans. One look at her and the mistresses of great houses had declined her services – especially once their husbands had seen her and expressed their enthusiasm that she be immediately employed.

Desperation had made her seek work in the French Quarter where the first job was offered by an angular black man wearing a white suit and gold teeth. He'd wanted a naked woman to suspend in a cage over the bar of a club he owned. 'A very special club,' he had told her. Two girls had wandered in dressed in black stockings, rubber corsets, and some kind of strap-like affair around their youthful breasts. Their nipples were painted gold. Shirley Anne had declined his offer.

'Come back if you're desperate,' he'd called out.

The entrance to the Catnip Club had looked the most inviting.

'There is just one problem,' Rene went on as he cupped her face in his hands.

Wide-eyed, she looked fearfully up into a face that seemed perpetually to be smiling, lashes like falls of soot around the brightness of his eyes.

'Your name,' he said softly.

He kissed her lips. A shiver went through her. It was as if the touch of his mouth had frozen out the memory of the man she had left behind.

'My name?' Her voice quivered as she breathed in the smell of him.

'The name Shirley. It is not a suitable name for a singer at the Catnip Club, *ma chérie*.'

He cocked his head to one side, a thoughtful look in his eyes.

'That is it, of course. Sheree. A mixture of Shirley and *chérie*. My dear. My dear one. How does that suit you?'

The butterflies in her belly were going crazy now. She could only nod, her eyes bright with excitement as she gazed at the man who had offered her a future.

'And I sing with the band?'

At the exact moment he answered, the sound of a slow-playing blues trombone came up from the club below and was joined by the higher notes of an equally sad trumpet.

Rene swayed, eyes half closed as the music drifted up into the room.

'They're real good,' she said. She meant it. She only hoped with all her heart that her voice would do them justice.

Rene opened his eyes. There was a look of reverence in them. His voice was low; sincere. 'Max and his band are good. Max is the best horn player there is. It's because there's a sadness in him.'

Chapter 3

Everyone had gone home and Max was alone and pretending he was somewhere else when Stacey, Rene's wife found him.

Hell, he thought to himself, and pretended he hadn't seen her. Instead, he sat himself down on the stage where the darkness was deepest, closed his eyes and lost his soul in his music.

The wail of his trumpet seemed to weave around the legs of the upturned chairs and dance a little with what remained of the cigarette smoke. It also clung to the Art-Deco mirrors along with the chips of blood-red glass that were fashioned into wild fruit decorating the frames. In turn the fruit clung to the figures of naked naiades that represented the seasons and the passions of men. Rome and Athens had given birth to such manifestations, and yet, like everything else, world over, they didn't seem out of place in the rich, thick pudding that was New Orleans.

'Feeling that sad, huh?'

Like a tall, sleek lily, she leaned against a pillar and sucked on her cigarette holder. With sultry eyes that looked as if they had seen everything, yet wanted to see more, she studied the big black man whose eyes were as sad as his music.

Along with his power to resist her, the melancholy tune came to an abrupt end. A spellbound Max let his gaze wander slowly up the pencil slim dress of shimmering stuff that almost seemed to tie Stacey's ankles together. As if it could. She made him feel helpless, but also incredibly randy; like some old billy goat. The thought both upset and annoyed him. He moaned and shut his eyes. Perhaps then she might disappear. But he knew she wouldn't; knew what she wanted; knew he was powerless to resist.

A slave to her will, he opened his eyes and turned his gaze slowly to her.

Her lips were bright red. Her eyes heavy with make-up. Hardly a hair of her blonde head showed from under the close-fitting cap she was wearing that accentuated her cheekbones and the sharp pertness of her chin.

'I'm feelin' pretty sad, but then you know that.' Max's voice had the same, dark melancholy about it as his trumpet playing.

'Want to tell me about it?' Stacey smiled provocatively. At the same time, her long, languid body seemed to wrap itself around the pillar she leaned against.

'You know about it.'

'Then perhaps you should tell me again. In private. Come on. I'll give you a lift home.'

Max had an urge to reject her offer. If he did, it would be the first time so far. But his need for someone to share his sadness was too much to bear. Slowly, he got to his feet. Almost with a sense of reverence, he put his instrument into its case and closed the lid.

As though she were leading him on some imagined leash, Stacey took him to her car which had dull mustard paintwork and a large white tyre clinging to its side. Like a limpet, or a clam, Max thought. Like her. Sticking real tight until needed elsewhere.

Just as he knew she would, she drove him to some place out near the sea where ramshackle huts clung to the sand between the swamp grass and the shoreline. It was a place that had become familiar to him since Emmeline had left.

She got out first, wrestled with the door of one of the huts, then went inside. Trumpet case in hand, he followed her.

The place was derelict and smelt of sea salt and leaf mould. Moonlight filtered through the windows and fell in patches on the sandy floor.

Max could see the shape of her, familiar as being Stacey Brabonne, Rene's wife. He put the thought of who she truly was from his mind. In this light she could be any woman. Any woman at all. But there was only one in his mind. As it was, her features were hidden in the shadows.

'Emmeline,' he whispered.

'You still think of me, honey?'

Stacey's voice had changed, just as Max knew it would.

'All the time.' His voice was little more than a whisper.

'Are you going to get it out, honey?'

Max stared into the shadows. Not once did the woman with him stray into the moonlight. Just as on other occasions, she would play her part.

'Yeah.' He sounded breathless because he had almost convinced himself that she really was someone else. But he gathered himself together, took his trumpet from its case and began to play.

His soul soared with the tune. Through half-closed eyes he could see her shape; the high breasts, slim waist, curving hips and long legs.

Yet he did not need to see to know that she was undressed. He could smell her. Female flesh, warm and getting warmer.

He willed himself to keep playing and willed her not to step into the moonlight and destroy the illusion. He closed his eyes and let her smell wash over him.

He dropped to his knees. She came closer then; ground her pelvis over his trumpet so that the sound became muted.

He smelt her sex, pungent, enticing. A woman's smell, though not the woman that was in his mind. But she knew that. Stacey knew that.

Not Stacey!

Think of Emmeline.

He thought of Emmeline as he put the trumpet down and stood up.

As slim fingers groped at his trouser buttons, he kept his eyes closed. Even as her lips closed over the ripe, pulsating end of his penis, he kept thinking of Emmeline, of her lips doing this and not some woman who wanted a real man for the night, not the sweet-smelling, neat-suited Rene, her husband.

He waited for the signal.

At first only her tongue licked over his flesh. Then her teeth nipped him gently. Then harder.

He grabbed at her head, pulled her to her feet.

She groaned and cried out as he pushed her against the

rough, wooden walls, his fingers digging into her haunches as he spread her legs and pushed himself into her.

He felt her buttocks clench, her hips jerk against him.

She hit him, yet when he retreated, she pulled him to her again.

The weight of his body pinioned her against the wall. No longer did he need to grasp her buttocks or her hips. She was helpless. His hands were free to cover her full, weighty breasts.

Each time he squeezed them, she cried out for him to stop.

'No!' she wailed. 'No!'

But he knew she didn't mean it. So he pulled on her nipples until it seemed they were twice the length they had been. Her cries turned to squeals.

The wet, warm flesh between her legs was open and inviting. His muscular buttocks clenched tightly as he plunged himself into her, sad it wasn't Emmeline, but glad it was someone.

He wanted to shoot his come into her, finish the natural process without having any regard to what she wanted.

But she was playing a part. And so was he. Until she came, he had to hold out.

'Oh, no!' she wailed again.

In turn, he covered each nipple with his mouth, bit at her until she wailed out again and again for him to stop. But he didn't stop. The scenario was always the same. She never really wanted him to stop.

The tip of his penis rammed through the neck of her womb. His length, his breadth filled her. She was speared on him like a trembling doll.

His pelvis thudded against her until Max perceived that familiar tightening of her stomach, the spasm as her body constricted around his rod.

Long and slow she wailed now, her body going limp as she yielded to a shattering orgasm.

'Emmeline,' Max whispered. 'Emmeline!'

At last, the orgasm he had held in check until she had come burst forth. He rammed his body against the now recumbent woman. She cried out as his weight squashed her against the rough wood of the shed wall which must surely have scratched her back. Would Rene notice? And did it matter if he did? It didn't matter to Max. Behind closed lids, he was imagining the woman he really wanted it to be.

'Emmeline!' And his voice echoed around the rotting wood and filtered out over the shingle and towards the sea.

Chapter 4

Emmeline wore silver shoes when she danced and, as she twirled and tapped her way across the stage of the Cotton Club in New York's Harlem, a few in the audience likened her speed to a bird in flight.

She was wearing white feathers on her head, and nothing more than a string of bananas around her waist, a tribute to Josephine Baker, a dancer she'd heard strutted her stuff at the Moulin Rouge in Paris. She laughed as she danced, a wild, infectious laugh that made her audience laugh too.

To wild applause, her legs kicked and her feet flashed, and all the time she sang a raucous song, the words of which made some laugh louder and others hide their blushes behind their hands.

Cheers and riotous clapping filled the club as she finished her dance and exited from beneath the bright lights. Sweat glistened on her face. By the time she regained the cooler confines of the back-stage dressing room, it was trickling down her neck, between her breasts and down her spine.

Lance was waiting for her in her room, his suave appearance marred by a lock of hair that fell decadently over his eyes.

Emmeline grimaced. Tonight she had a yearning to be alone. She had things to think about. Old problems to mull over. Her tone reflected her sullen mood.

'You've been drinking. What are you doing here?'

'Waiting for you.'

'You're a fool. And what's more you're an irresponsible fool.'

'I'm in love.'

As she eased the heavy silver earrings out from her lobes, she laughed and shook her head.

'Then you are a fool!' *And I should know*, she thought to herself. Suddenly, the pain she felt inside turned to anger.

Lance looked hurt, and seeing that made her feel powerful somehow. Here was someone to vent her anger on. There he was, an English earl or whatever, and he was in love with her, a girl from the deep south with dark brown skin and an offhand way with men.

He clasped his hands together, elbows resting on knees, face intensely anxious. 'You shame me, Emmeline. You call me a fool. But I can't help being foolish. I'm besotted with you. You know that.'

The loudness of her laughter hid her own pain. Her throat vibrated with the sound of it as she threw the silver earrings onto her dressing table where they landed with a heavy clunk.

It was one laugh too much.

'Damn it, Emmeline!'

He sprang to his feet.

'This is too much. You're right. I am a fool. A fool to hang around here!'

He made for the door, his old-fashioned opera cloak flying out behind him.

Suddenly, Emmeline felt regretful she had treated him so. After all, having an English lord enamoured of her went some way to healing the hurt she felt inside. Both her attitude and her tone of voice changed.

'Lance, darling. How can you leave me like this?' Her voice was as sweetly beguiling as thick treacle.

Fingers curled over door knob, Lance turned and looked at her.

'How can you leave me like this?' Emmeline said again, her voice more plaintive, tempting, as she eased the thin straps of her odd outfit off her shoulders. Smiling seductively, she reached behind her to release the last fastening. 'How can you possibly leave me like this?'

The string of wax fruit and its thin, silk bodice slid down over her body and lay in a heap around her ankles.

Underneath, she wore nothing except silk stockings held up by silver garters with small bells on the sides. Smiling triumphantly, she held her arms out to either side of her and shook her body. The bells on her legs tinkled. So did the ones that hung from her nipples.

Because her breasts were small, no one ever noticed that her nipples were unusually pert by virtue of the tiny silver bells that hung from them. Piercing had taken place when she had been younger – about the same time her ears had been done.

Every man she had ever met had been charmed by them, keen to look closer and set the sweet chimes in motion with his finger, his tongue or something much larger.

Her gaze fixed on the captivated Englishman, she took

her feet out of the nest of bananas and, after kicking it to one side, stood with her legs slightly apart.

'Do you like my tune?' she murmured, and shook her body again.

This time another bell joined in.

Lance gasped. Sweat broke out on his forehead.

Besides having bells on her garters and jingling from her bosom, a glint of silver shone from between Emmeline's legs. Finding her pierced nipples had enhanced sexual pleasure, she had immediately imagined how her clitoris might respond to extra stimulation. Accordingly, a piercing had occurred there too.

'Well?' she asked again, delighting in the fact that the look and the sound of her could make a man turn white and cause him to sweat like a horse.

Mouth opening and shutting like a goldfish, Lance continued to stare, his breathing coming in quick, short gasps.

Emmeline shook again and the bells jingled. Just as she had danced before an audience, she now danced before him. But this was so different.

Her brown limbs glistened, complimenting the glint of the silver bells that sang a merry tune when she moved.

Lance sank trembling to his knees, his eyes never leaving her body, his lower lip quivering and damp.

At last her dance stopped. She stood before him.

'Worship me,' she hissed, 'Worship me as I should be worshipped.'

There was a look of ecstasy in her eyes as she gazed down on him.

His breath stirred her cluster of thick, black pubic hair. Lance's mouth hung open, but no words came out.

'Go on,' she urged. 'Worship me.'

She shook her hips. The bell that hung from her clitoris tinkled and glinted.

Like a man whose will is no longer his own, a limpness came upon the honourable lord. The gap between his mouth and her pubes narrowed. His tongue snaked out of his mouth and tapped at the bell.

Emmeline laughed, opened her legs a little wider.

Now his tongue prodded and paddled over the slippery wet flesh of her sex. Above him, she moaned, raised her arms above her head and stretched her body. As she did so, the bells that hung from her nipples rested against her flesh, their peal silenced whilst the man kneeling before her paid her homage.

Delicate tracings of sensation began where his tongue travelled. Emmeline made long, low sounds like the contented purr of a cat. She even looked like a cat stretched as she was; a lean feline giving nothing in return for the pleasure given her.

Her hips swayed slightly as the sensations increased.

His hands caressed her thighs as his tongue caressed her sex.

Aware she was becoming aroused, Lance tempered her progress by transferring his attention and his tongue to the crease where her right leg joined her trunk. He did the same to the left.

Clitoris aching for attention, she moaned, then shook her hips so that the small bell rang, demanding his return.

Poor Lance. His will was not his own. The bell summoned him back and he was too weak to refuse.

Knowing her time was near, he cupped her buttocks in

his hands and sunk his tongue back into her cleft. She began to rock backwards and forwards against his face. As she did so, the bells on her body began to peel in unison.

Suddenly, her whole body shook as if in time to some unheard music. Eyes closed, she moved to the tempo she heard only in her mind, its tones, its melody saturating her body. Like music, it reached a crescendo, then fell, softening, breaking into many different pieces until the last note had sounded.

A tune in my head, an earl at my feet, she thought as she eyed the top of his head through narrowed eyes. *If only Max could see me now. If only Rene hadn't come between us.*

Chapter 5

Prisms of colour flashed from the tight-fitting cap that Sheree wore that first night she sang in the Catnip Club.

The cap was of blue satin encrusted with crystals, and because it hid her hair and sparkled like some angel's halo around her head, it made her eyes seem greener, her cheekbones higher, and her lips as glossy as satin.

Before she started singing, the band had belted out a fast and furious number that had sent feet tapping and couples dancing crazy concoctions of Charleston and sheer tribal jumping all around the dance floor.

When she started to sing, her voice crept along with the sound of the sax and the soulful sobbing of Max's trumpet. Her hips began to sway, her shoulders to shrug alternately in time with the music.

Emotion and pathos mixed with sexuality in the same way as Sheree's voice mixed with the growl of the groaning brass.

Infused with the sensuality of her voice, the couples on the dance floor changed tempo, bodies seeming to fuse into one, undulating as they moved slowly around the floor.

'Man, you make your mamma cry,
Cos you don't come round,
You leave her high and dry,
Don't come round and love her,
Anymore . . .'

Just like the dancing couples, Sheree's own body swayed suggestively to the music.

'Come and love her,
Come and feel her,
Take this body, and do whatever you wanna . . .'

Eyes half closed, Sheree clasped her breasts as she sang, then ran her hands down to her waist and over her belly.

Slowly, as if the hands belonged to someone else, she thrust her pelvis backwards and forwards, bending her knees, opening her legs slightly so that the multicoloured silk dress she wore shimmered like the cool greens and blues of the sea washing over her body.

As she moved, she relished the cool feel of the silk and the mix of thick smoke that curled up between her legs.

Those not dancing listened spellbound as her voice plunged to deep bass, then lifted, climbing the scale like a slow, sexual arousal.

Although her eyes were half closed and her mind and body immersed in her song, Sheree was very aware that Rene sat at the bar like a man carved from wood. *Like a cigar-store Indian*, she thought, and felt as though she were singing and moving just for him.

There were others in the audience who looked at her in a

similar way to Rene, her image clear in their minds despite the thick curtain of cigar smoke.

But like her voice, Sheree let her mind wander around the room. And, also like her voice, her mind seeped into the minds of others.

In the past she had been afraid of what she had seen in men's minds. Just lately, fear had changed to amusement.

One man, his face aglow with smug pleasure, sat holding the hand of the woman with him. They were both in their late thirties and every so often he would pat the woman's hand and smile at her reassuringly.

Each time he turned his eyes back to Sheree, she saw a vision. In his mind, she was like a wax doll lying quietly in a box, swathed in layers of crisp, white tissue paper. She saw him put the box up on end and slowly peel each piece of paper away until she was exposed; completely naked!

She saw the rest of his vision. Saw him move to a gramophone, wind it up, then place the needle onto the record.

The music on the record and that in the club were one and the same. In the club she was fully clothed as she moved, but the doll in the man's mind was completely naked and the dance unbelievably lewd. She blinked and the vision disappeared. Her gaze went elsewhere.

Vibrating with song, her body swayed. She spread her fingers and fanned at the air as her voice and the music reached fever pitch.

As the music touched her very soul, desire was born deep in her body and slowly spread outwards like the rays of a very warm sun. Errol, then Rene came into her mind; Errol's brown body, naked, aroused and undulating with hers until they were like two hungry snakes both waiting for the chance to devour the other.

And Rene.

Through the curling smoke, her gaze went back to Rene who was still standing at the bar. His wife, Stacey, was with him. The blonde's sultry eyes held her gaze and a slow smile played around the bright red lips.

Images from Stacey's mind flashed into her own. Because of the nature of Stacey's thoughts, a surprised flush spread over her face.

In the mind of Rene's wife, she saw herself sitting astride Rene as Stacey instructed her on how best to satisfy her husband. She could clearly see the blonde's hand on her buttocks, pushing her down onto him, urging her to ride him harder, to do better in order to satisfy him.

Face reddening, she dragged her gaze away. She sang the last notes of the song. It finished and Max was by her side.

'Ya hit the mark, baby,' Max muttered in her ear as she took the applause of the crowd. 'Same time, same place later.'

Before she could respond, his thick fingers were already in action and his trumpet was wailing again.

Intrigued by what she had seen in the minds she had read, her gaze immediately went back to the man who employed her. Rene gestured for her to join him. Stacey stood languidly at his side, a faint smile on her lips, an unfathomable gleam in her eyes.

Unwilling to meet Stacey's gaze, Sheree concentrated on acknowledging the appreciative smiles and positive comments of the customers as she squeezed her slim hips between tables.

'Marvellous, my dear. Simply marvellous.'

'The best voice we've had here in many a day.'

'Beautiful voice. Beautiful woman.'

Some kissed her hand. Some said with their eyes what they did not say with their voice.

Some touched her body, but only as if by accident when it was obviously nothing of the kind.

The bar itself was a beige marble affair decorated with orange and brown diagonal lines. Mirrors lined the shelves on which stood rows of bottles, everything the barman could possibly need to make every cocktail ever invented.

Rene kissed her on each cheek. 'Wonderful, *ma chérie. Superbe!*'

'Good for you, honey,' Stacey added, her look as sharp and disarming as any well-honed knife. 'You look special and sound special. Drip with promise in fact.'

She exchanged a swift look with Rene and it seemed as if she were about to say something. But she didn't. Sheree caught the hint of warning in his eyes.

'Curb your enthusiasm, *mon amour*. We don't want to frighten our little Sheree off before she has fully come to know us.'

They smiled, held each other's gaze for a moment and laughed lightly.

Sheree joined in, though realised she was not supposed to be privy to their innermost thoughts. And yet, she already had an inkling of how dark their thoughts and their actions might be.

Stacey laughed louder, slid her arm around Sheree's waist and kissed her cheeks in the same way Rene had done.

'Oh, I think our little songbird here will get to know us real well in time. In fact, I think she's gonna fit in with me and you like a slice of pastrami between two slices of rye. Ain't that right, Sheree, little darling?'

Sheree paused before she answered, her eyes wide and mouth slightly open as she looked at Stacey's smiling face. By itself what Stacey had said could easily be taken two ways. But, added to the fact that her hand had slid down Sheree's back and was now caressing and squeezing one buttock, Sheree was left in no doubt of its true meaning.

Chapter 6

'You want her, don't you, Rene, my darling.'

Rene and his wife were sitting at a table, a bottle of good burgundy between them. The room was small, but with a high ceiling, a secret place whose only door led to a staircase which in turn led to their apartment below.

Rene barely acknowledged his wife's comment. His pulse was racing. A blood vessel on his forehead was throbbing just beneath a lock of dark, silky hair. His eyes did not leave the sheet of glass which, to him and his wife sitting in the small room, was a window. To the unsuspecting young woman in the room on the other side, it seemed merely to be a mirror.

Sheree took off the clothes she had worn in the club and, stripping down to only her chemise, strolled out onto the balcony, a beautiful French inspired affair so typical of the better buildings in the Quarter.

Lights blinked from windows and the sky seemed to hang like a purple, muslin scarf just a few inches above the buildings.

Traffic had ceased in the streets and squares, yet Sheree still perceived a hum of life throbbing around the city, sleeping just below the surface until morning when it woke, and evening when it truly reached its climax.

Taking deep gulps of air, she leaned against the ironwork and looked at the buildings opposite and then along the facade of the building in which she lodged.

Tall windows beneath ornate plasterwork looked out into the night. Unlike her room, the one next door had no balcony. As she studied it, she perceived a small glimmer of light shining through a gap in the blinds.

She frowned. Wasn't she the only tenant on this floor? That's what she had been given to understand from her suave, sophisticated employer.

Rene and Stacey had the rooms downstairs; a luxurious spread that filled three floors. There was even a basement down below that, though, according to Rene, it was unused as such.

'I only use it for personal hobbies,' he had told her.

Of course, the room next door could also be used by them, and yet Sheree could not recall there being a door into it from the passageway outside. There was only her door, the rest nothing but blank walls. Unless, of course, there was a private staircase from the dwelling beneath, or even the dwelling to the rear or side of them.

She shrugged. Why worry? Her gaze went back to the city and the night. The air was not as oppressive as usual, and its freshness made her feel light-headed. Excited. And why shouldn't she be? She was young, and she looked like being successful. What more could she ask for?

Stretching her arms high above her head, she walked back into her room where the windows also stretched between the ceiling and the floor.

After slipping off her underwear, her garters and stockings would normally have followed. But she caught a glimpse of herself in the mirror and stopped.

The mirror had a gilt frame of flying cherubs and naked goddesses. A bracket candle holder stood out from each side of it, its base dripping with crystal lozenges.

At first, the sight of her naked body held her attention, the breasts firm and pert, the areolae large, plush and pink. Her ribs curved down to a narrow waist. Her hips flared, but not hugely, and the naked flesh above her garters shone like the softest of silk.

Her body and the room looked like a beautiful picture, complimented by the ornate gilt frame which she felt compelled to touch.

'Pretty,' she murmured, her finger running over the fat little bottom of one pert cherub.

Her eyes went back to herself. The mirror was large. She stepped away from it and eyed the full length of her body. Without being touched, her nipples hardened and became larger as her blood warmed and rushed through her veins.

She ran her hand down over her belly and lightly touched the nest of dark hair that spilled out from between her legs.

She turned her bottom towards the mirror and looked at her reflection over her shoulder. She smiled. Why was it that she looked more naked, her buttocks more vulnerable with just her stockings on.

Giggling to herself, she turned round and faced the mirror again. It was still the same. The stockings accentuated her nakedness.

Her giggle subsided. Something about looking at herself ignited thoughts of Errol. He had often gazed on her and told her she was beautiful and incredibly sexy. And then he had reached for her. Suddenly, she missed him.

Just as he would have done, she cupped her breasts, squeezed them, and slid her index fingers over her nipples.

She moaned just as if it were Errol doing it.

Half closing her eyes, she ran her hands down over her body, appreciating the firmness of her own flesh, the silkiness of her own skin. She turned, back to the mirror, crossed her arms across her front, brought her hands over her shoulders and caressed her back. In the mirror, it looked as if it might be other fingers, not hers, spreading over her flesh.

'I wish . . .' she murmured, but could put no name to what she desired.

Her eyes followed the curve of her back, the roundness of her bottom. She let her hands slide down her ribs, her waist, over hips and onto her buttocks.

The touch of her own hands, her own fingers clasping, digging, clutching, then releasing was good, though not as good as having someone else do it. All the same, hot flames seemed to lick over her skin, and yet it still felt cool and soft.

Through narrowed eyes she admired the full firmness of her buttocks, one nestling against the other like a large, ripe peach. How soft they were, yet how firm.

My own body is enticing me, she thought, *and I cannot resist it*.

Her breath came in quick snatches. There was a heaviness in her abdomen and a ticklishness between her thighs that made her want to thrust her hips and curve her back.

'Not yet,' she breathed, her eyes wide as she eyed each

buttock and dared herself to explore her body as she had never explored it before.

One hand on each cheek, she probed cautiously into the crack between. Spreading her fingers wide, she pulled one buttock away from the other. Her face became warm as she took in the details of what lay between them. Like a daisy, she thought. A small, mauve daisy that dilates and constricts at will.

One finger strayed to tap at its petals, to push into its centre.

Her muscles tightened over the intruder like lips sucking in some delicious fruit.

Sheree watched herself through blurred eyes, her body on fire, reacting to both what she saw and what she was doing.

Letting her buttocks go, she turned round, lips parted and a pinkness blossoming in her cheeks. Eyes glittering and tongue stroking her bottom lip, she slid her hand between her legs. A satin wetness transferred from her hidden flesh to her fingers. She pushed her pelvis backwards and forwards and shuddered as electrifying sensations poured out with her juices.

And yet it was not enough. Her body was on fire, tense with a desire that was like a pouring tap, or a cascade of water falling into a lake. She was that lake and desire was filling her up, threatening to flood. It was too much to be placated by her own hand. She wanted someone else's. She closed her eyes and tried to imagine.

'Errol,' she moaned.

But Errol was not here. He was back where she had grown up, lamenting her departure but, no doubt, sowing his wild oats before they got too stale.

Sheree's eyes flitted swiftly around the room. She had to have someone. Something.

Ornate and as tasteful inside as it was out, the furniture and decorations of the room seemed to whirl and burn with the frenzy of her searching.

There was a bed with a golden brocade cover. White linen drapes hung from a brass and blue bead coronet above its head. Cream closets decorated with ormolu fronds and sweeps, all gilded with pale green and gold, stood against a wall. Tall gas lamps on heavy tripods hissed in each corner. There was a low chest of drawers that would not have looked out of place in the court of the Sun King, Louis the Fourteenth of France. And there were chairs of gold brocade, their legs braced on ball and claw feet, the claws themselves gilded like the rest of the furniture. There were also ornaments; china, glass, bronze and brass.

There was also a five foot high statue just to the left of the window. It was the old, black footman sort holding a tray in front of him on which drinks would sometimes be put.

Breathing rapidly, Sheree, still wearing only her stockings, went across to him and quickly removed the tray.

Her eyes opened wide. A handful of bent, hard fingers had been exposed.

Breasts heaving, she got astride the spread hand. Two fingers stood up proud of the rest. Sheree eased herself down onto them, murmuring with delight as, unyielding, they pushed their way into her.

Carefully at first, she began to ride him, her eyes half closed and a low moan escaping her throat.

His palm, like his fingers, was hard against her sex and

was formed of high plateaus and low indentations that issued just the right pressure against the rest of her erogenous flesh.

Sighing with delight, she wriggled a little on his hard hand so that, soon, she could almost forget he had no life. No warmth. He was only very hard and always available.

As she rode him, she leaned forward so that her breasts slapped the hardness of his little face.

Despite his eyes having a serious look, there was an open expression to the mock human face, and yet he seemed a little sad.

'Ooow,' Sheree moaned as she stroked his cold cheek. 'Perhaps you would like to enjoy this too. Perhaps that would make you happy.'

Taking hold of one nipple between finger and thumb, she pushed it into his gaping mouth. She gasped as the warmth of her nipple met the coldness of his mouth. Strangely enough, she could almost believe his lips closed on it.

As one set of fingers manipulated her other nipple, a long finger of her other hand went back behind her to feel again the tight flower that blossomed between her buttocks.

What a man! He wasn't complaining or demanding that she do this or that to him. He was doing exactly what she wanted, his hard fingers and mouth untiring and uncomplaining.

As her juice ran over his fingers and dripped onto the floor, she threw her arms around him and hugged his head against her breast.

Rene and Stacey exchanged silent looks. A knowing smile played around Stacey's mouth. Rene's eyes seemed to burn with white heat.

'I told you I was right.'

Stacey's voice was even more husky than usual.

Rene swallowed and licked at his lips. He was having trouble even speaking.

'*Oui*. You were right. Even so, we must wait until the moment is right.'

Stacey's smile did not waver. Even as she slid her dress from one shoulder, it remained exactly the same.

Moving closer to him, she extricated one breast, ran her finger around its areole, then pulled on her nipple until it stood hard and proud from her breast.

Rene watched impassively, though desire danced in his eyes.

Stacey picked up her wine glass and refilled it. She came close to him, dipped her nipple into the dark, red liquid, then sighed with satisfaction as her husband sucked both it and her nipple into his mouth.

Lips parted, Stacey murmured with pleasure as her husband's tongue licked and prodded at her succulent teat. Behind her closed eyelids she could still see the girl in the next room, her body racked with desire.

'I wonder who Errol is?' she murmured before dipping her nipple into the wine and again offering it to her husband.

Chapter 7

Errol sat on the porch of the place he'd shared with Shirley Anne, his head in his hands. 'I'm going to find her,' he said softly. 'I ain't lettin' her go that easy.'

His brother, Jim, looked at him soulfully. 'P'raps she don't wanna be found.'

'I don't care. I'm still gonna go lookin'.'

Jim walked with him to the bus stop. He didn't tell him he was a fool. But Errol knew the look in his eyes said it all, so he made a great effort not to look at his brother.

'Take care,' Jim called as the bus moved off.

Errol nodded and smiled faintly.

Somehow, he couldn't accept that Shirley Anne had gone all the way to New Orleans. Of course, she'd talked about going there some day, of leaving the place she'd been born in and taking up some real, good job in town. But he'd taken that to mean Le Farge, a place of about 60,000 souls just fifteen miles away. That's where he was going first. If he couldn't find her there, then he would surely be convinced he should go looking in New Orleans. Till then, he would stay in Le Farge and do his best to find her.

When he got there, it was midday and the sun was hot,

and the air clung to his skin like sugar water.

Errol took off his jacket. Not that he got that much cooler. His shirt stuck to his skin and his trousers clung tightly to his body.

He started asking around as to whether anyone had seen a good-looking girl with green eyes asking for work. He asked at the big houses where domestic servants were always wanted. No one recalled someone looking like her.

By the time he'd tramped around a good few big places, he was dog tired and ready to quit for the day. He was also hungry, and asking about Shirley Anne had made him want her just like he used to. He felt no shame at that. Errol had always had a good appetite as far as sex was concerned. It came to him as naturally as drinking or eating. None of them were bad habits, he told himself. Not like gambling or drinking. *Just think*, he thought. *If sex was whisky, I'd most likely be a drunk!*

Despite the anxiety of his mission, the thought made him laugh, and laughing made his footsteps that much lighter.

The afternoon went fast and the sun was hanging red and heavy in the west.

The last house he tried was a big place with gables that were common in towns, but more usually found in the northern states rather than the south.

Thick lace hung at the windows and a widow's walk ran around the major part of the roof.

'One more time,' Errol muttered to himself. 'One more time.'

Slinging his coat over his shoulder, he opened a white painted gate and strolled purposefully up the garden path. As he did so, he studied the big windows that were half

Anything Goes

hidden because big, angular yellow shades were pulled out over them like hooded eyelids.

As he studied them, he chanced to notice a slight movement, a shifting of a curtain. The moment he glanced in that direction, it dropped back into position.

Shunning the idea that he should go round the back to the trade entrance, he rapped firmly at a thick black knocker formed into the face of a leering, tipsy-looking Bacchus.

The sun beat on his feet as he waited. It beat on the garden too, the green of the grass now seeming to visibly discolour as the last vestige of water was sucked from the soil.

Someone answering was a slow process. He would have turned and gone, but in-built stubbornness took a tight hold. He wanted to find Shirley Anne. He also wanted to find a bed for the night and some food to fill the gap in his guts.

Vaguely aware of a soft footfall, he pressed his ear closer to the door then, just before it opened, he stood up real straight and prepared to ask questions of some offhand butler or maid.

The door slid smoothly open and a smell of camellias seemed to tumble out into the hot smell of day's end.

'Do come in, sir.'

Errol had come to expect servants in positions of authority, such as butlers and housekeepers, to be getting on in years, their status achieved over a period of time.

But this butler was around his own age, shiny of face and bright of eye, his nose straight, and a tilt of chin that hinted at arrogance. He was also around six feet tall, roughly the same as Errol was himself.

'I think you've got this wrong. I was only going to ask—'

'My mistress will answer anything you care to ask.'

The servant's face remained almost expressionless, yet Errol fancied he saw an excited sparkle in his eyes.

Errol found himself walking on black and white tiles through a reception hall with yellow painted walls. Vaudeville posters hung in ebony frames from the walls. He'd never heard of anyone doing that before.

A thick clutch of pampas grass sprouted from a blue and white vase that must have been at least four feet high. There was a lightness, a brightness about the place that Errol felt he should have expected judging from its outside appearance, and yet it still came as something of a surprise; like a present. Or new shoes.

'This way.'

The voice of the servant interrupted his thoughts.

'Nice place.' Errol smiled in an over-friendly way at the butler, or whatever he was.

The man did not comment. He just smiled serenely and directed Errol through a door into a spacious room where French doors opened out onto a bountiful garden.

Errol swore softly. The doors seemed to form one complete side of the room. Bright foliage formed a background to white door frames and mint-green walls.

'I need another man to help Pierre. My demands on him are quite . . . phenomenal.'

The woman's voice took Errol by surprise. He looked to the door, but it had closed and the servant had gone.

'Please. Come through into the conservatory.'

Errol turned his face back to where the smell of camellias and rich vegetation hung like a thick curtain.

Ferns tickled his face as he went to where the voice was coming from.

He stopped in his tracks when he saw her.

Her hair was very red and fell in a luxuriant mane over her snowy-white shoulders.

She was lying on a lounger that was full of cushions and stood on cast-iron legs.

She smiled when she saw him and her eyes sparkled in the same way Shirley Anne's had sparkled. On top of that, they were exactly the same colour.

A silky kimono-type garment decorated with brightly coloured birds and huge flowers was all she appeared to be wearing. It barely covered her body and slid easily down from her shoulders.

One breast, one nipple peeped out from over the cluster of silk that she held to herself.

He could have left then and there, but he didn't. Suddenly, finding Shirley Anne didn't seem quite so important. Besides, this woman might know something. Apart from the colour of her skin, she even looked a bit like Shirley Anne, although she was a good few years older.

'Well?' she asked with a raising of her arched eyebrows. 'Do you want a job, or don't you?'

The questions Errol had meant to ask seemed to melt away like so much crushed ice. He couldn't help that his gaze kept dropping to her nipple, and he also couldn't help the stirring in his loins.

'I think I do,' he answered, and licked his lips.

The silk rustled as the red-haired woman rearranged herself. As she did so, he saw her snowy, flat belly and a thick bush of bright red hair licking like a flame between her smooth, white thighs.

He sucked in his breath, aware that his stomach was

knotting and the one-eyed snake that lay in his trousers was raising its head and getting ready to strike.

Would it be so bad if he stayed awhile?

The woman's eyes widened with her smile as she slowly gathered up the folds of soft silk and eased it back over one rounded hip.

Errol's eyes widened, his breath coming in short sharp gasps that were almost hurting his throat. But nothing could hurt as much as the pressure of his cock against the buttons of his trousers. There was just no room left in them anymore. It had to come out.

His fingers went to the buttons.

'That's it, big boy,' murmured the smiling woman. 'Let Amber see what you've got there.'

Amber. That was her name. It hardly seemed to matter. She was a woman, and he'd already been getting hard thinking about Shirley Anne. This woman had aided his erection, her flashing her milky white flesh like that. *Now*, thought Errol, *she can abet it getting a bit harder and a lot more satisfied.*

As his cock leapt out from his open trousers, Amber raised herself up on one elbow, her eyes gleaming and her fleshy tongue cruising hungrily over her lips.

'Come closer.'

She was hot. He could tell she was real hot, because her voice was more husky than it had been.

Resting his hands on his hips, he went to her, his baton waving proudly from side to side as he did so.

He stopped when its tip was just a few inches from her nose. It amused him to see her go almost cross-eyed as she took in his impressive measurements.

'Just the sort of tool I could do with around here,' she said. She tapped at the end of his cock and laughed softly as it jerked forcefully and his testicles hugged more closely around its base.

'Let me try it,' she said as he reached for her breasts. 'Lie down on the floor.'

Errol had always been used to taking the lead with most women – except Shirley Anne that is, whose appetite for sex was as expansive as his own. Amber, it appeared, was another woman who liked to make demands.

'OK,' he said smiling, and lay himself down on a red and blue carpet that felt warm and soft against his back.

'Pull your pants down a bit.'

Her words were now hard to distinguish from her heavy breathing. Hearing her sound like that made Errol just as horny. He duly obliged and slid his trousers down to his knees. In doing so, his prick stood proudly from his body, its base covered by a forest of unruly blue-black hair.

'Lovely,' he heard Amber breathe. 'Just what I'm looking for. Exactly what I'm looking for.'

'Now,' she added. 'Turn over. Let me look at your ass.'

Her demand surprised him. So did the word she used. Wanton she might be, but in his experience even wanton women of her social class did not use common expressions. *Vive la différence*, he thought, and duly turned over.

He heard the rustle of silk as she slid off the lounger. He saw her feet disappear and heard the silk rustle again as she bent to examine his behind.

Earlier his penis had pained him because it was hardening against his trousers. Now it was paining him even more as it hardened against the carpet and the floor. Just the thought of her gazing on his nakedness was enlarging his erection.

If he thought that was painful, what she did next sent shivers of mixed pain and delight through his body.

A soft hand and caressing fingers swept over each buttock in turn. Then she lay her hand flat upon both and slid it down until her fingers were touching the rear of his scrotum.

He groaned and closed his eyes tightly. This was too much. Only the discomfort of his penis being trapped between him and the floor stopped him from ejaculating. If she continued like this, her red and blue carpet would have an added splash of white on it.

'A firm bottom, yet such skin. Soft. Like satin.'

Just when he thought he could stand it no more, the door opened. The man who had shown him in glanced briefly at him before setting a silver tray of drinks down on a small table.

'Thank you, Pierre. Leave us. For now.'

Errol did not see any look pass between them, yet he sensed the servant had paused and, in that moment, some sort of understanding had flashed between him and his mistress.

'Come. Get to your feet and sit here beside me. You're hot. You smell of sweat. Like a horse, and like a horse you probably need to drink.'

Clutching at his trousers and embarrassed to see his member had not declined in size, Errol struggled to his feet.

Amber tossed her red mane over her shoulder and smiled. 'Don't be shy. Come on. Sit here.' She patted the place beside her. 'And take off your shirt. It's sticking to you. Your trousers first.'

Anything Goes

Wide-eyed, she stared as she sipped her drink, her mouth smiling appreciatively as he removed his trousers, socks and shoes. The urge to cover his privates was strong, yet he sensed she would not like that. Better to flaunt it, he decided. As if it had acquired a mind of its own, his member flaunted itself. Head glistening, it peered out from beneath the cotton of his shirt. Somehow he felt even more vulnerable wearing just a shirt than he would have if he'd been completely naked.

'Come on,' she said again, sensing his hesitation. 'You're beautiful. Desirable. Why shouldn't a red-blooded woman like me enjoy looking at a specimen like you?'

She reached for the glass that remained on the tray.

'Come on. Take it off. Relax. And you can have this.' She held out the drink.

Suddenly, it all seemed so perfectly natural. Pride replaced Errol's bashfulness as he peeled his sticky shirt away from his body.

He stretched his lean torso as he did so, knowing his stomach muscles would flatten and make his chest seem more muscled, his cock more noticeable.

'My!' Amber exclaimed as his prick jerked upwards. 'Just like I said. A beautiful tool. Real useful I bet too.'

Errol took the glass as he sat beside her. The freshness of mint and lemonade ran cool into his throat. His eyes stayed fixed on Amber who smiled as he sipped.

'Go on,' she urged. 'Drink your fill. Cool yourself down.'

As he drank, he felt her fingers trace patterns on his thigh.

'That's nice,' he said. 'And this is real nice you giving me this drink. But I've got to tell you, I'm not really looking for a job?'

Her smile faded. She raised her eyebrows.

'Are you allergic to work, then, big boy?'

'No, ma'am,' he said, shaking his head emphatically lest she think him a bum. 'I'm looking for Shirley Anne, my girl. She left early in the morning a month or so ago, and I'm out trying to find her. If I could show you her picture . . .'

He slid his hand to his hip as though he were just about to take something from his pocket.

He laughed at his own stupidity and slapped his thigh. 'I must be going crazy. I forgot I haven't got my pants on.'

Her smile seemed to widen. *She's waiting for me*, he told himself. *And why shouldn't I give her what she wants? There's my ramrod all ready for action, and there's her fair giving me the signal to fire.*

He smiled broadly and, although he was feeling a little woozy, he gulped back the rest of his drink. Better get on with it. Do it to her, then hit the trail again, even if it meant New Orleans.

Was it his imagination, or was her smile broadening, spreading across her face until all he could see was her mouth, a gigantic thing that seemed to be devouring everything else around it?

Something hit hard against his face, or at least it felt as though it did, yet it did not hurt. It merely made him fall sideways, despite his attempts to keep his balance. His head sank into a cushion and, although he still had it in his mind to make love to Amber, such desire was overcome by a sudden need to sleep.

Chapter 8

Dreams came and went, one dream finishing, then fading into another; a patchwork of odd occurrences and odder sensations.

Some seemed almost real. Some were too crazy to be real. In his dream he was naked, but that was no big deal. Doesn't everyone have dreams of being naked, walking down a busy street, and no one seemingly aware of their embarrassment?

And yet, he half suspected it was not a dream. His flesh felt cool and it wasn't unpleasant. Was there actually somewhere in Louisiana that was cool? He'd be a rich man if he could bottle it and sell it on.

A murmur of voices came and went. Hands touched him. Something was around his neck, his wrists and his ankles. Whatever it was felt tight; heavy.

Reality crept into the dream when he felt his weight hanging on his arms. Something was dragging them upwards until the soles of his feet barely kept contact with the floor.

Suddenly, he was afraid. Sleep was retreating, and yet the dream stayed with him.

Squinting at first, he opened his eyes, but saw nothing.

All was darkness. Complete and utter blackness.

Panic replaced fear. Had he gone blind whilst asleep? Was that possible?

The urge to rub at his eyes was incredibly strong. Rubbing the sleep away was a sure way of seeing things straight. But he couldn't do that. Try as he might, he could not drag his arms down.

Perhaps I am still asleep, he thought. *Perhaps this blackness is all part of the dream.*

He struggled, made a huge effort to bring his arms down, but felt the bite of cold metal around his wrists.

What's happening? The question was the only thing that filled his head, and he badly wanted it answering.

Perhaps if he could walk away from this dream . . .

He tried to move his legs. Nothing happened. The same cold metal that held his wrists also held his ankles.

Am I still dreaming?

A dream had become a nightmare. What else would it be if you couldn't walk away from it? This was a nightmare with no setting, no form. So far, it had also been silent. He tried to shout, felt himself shaking his head, straining against something that covered his mouth.

In that awful moment, he felt as though he had slipped into a great black void. Was he dead?

Terror racked his brain, made his body shiver.

Realisation, frightening but somehow enlightening, suddenly came to him as his fingers intertwined some way above him. He was restrained, in complete darkness, and something was over his mouth. It was as plain as that.

But how long had he been here, and what was it all about?

'Errol. Get a hold of yourself.' It really sounded as if he were saying it, and yet he was sure he could neither hear the words nor move his mouth.

A trickle of sweat coursed down between his shoulder blades and trickled slowly down his spine.

His ears strained to hear the faintest of sound. He heard a rustling, thought it might be rats, then realised it was the sound of running water. It figured. These old places were built on land reclaimed from the bayous, the water rerouted to flow away from the foundations. Yet it never went away entirely. That was the glory of this state, especially around the delta. You were never really very far from the Mississippi.

He heard footsteps, then the grating of a key in a lock. Part of him felt glad to hear something. Another part was fearful.

He saw the oil lamp first, then the smooth, aquiline features of the silent Pierre, his nostrils looking more flared and much blacker beneath the shadows thrown by the flickering light.

Amber entered behind him. She was also carrying an oil lamp.

Errol's heart leapt in his chest. Inwardly, he knew he should be scared, but just seeing someone after being alone in that darkness was enough to make him glad. Nothing she could do to him was comparable to that.

He attempted to speak to her, but his voice was no more than a muted rumble behind the leather pad that covered his mouth.

Clenching and unclenching his fists, he attempted to break free of the bonds that held his arms tightly above his head. His body swayed. His flesh glistened with sweat.

The smiling Amber placed her hand flat on his chest, her fingers playful among his chest hair.

'There's no point in struggling, my beautiful man.' She raised her eyebrows as she smiled and ran her hand down over his ribs.

He yearned to scratch the ticklish sensation her fingers left in their wake. From her eyes, he realised she knew that. Pleasure, he understood, could be tortuous if used in a certain way.

Amber was no longer looking him in the face. She was studying his body, her eyes and her hands exploring him as though he were no more than a bolt of cloth, or a piece of furniture.

Pierre stood behind her, the light from the lamp he was holding throwing her shadow over Errol's body.

At first, Errol assumed Pierre's eyes too were exploring his flesh. But then he realised it was Amber that Pierre was watching. There was passion in his eyes, an oscillating flame that hinted at unhealthy obsession.

Errol trembled as Amber's long, white fingers burrowed into his pubic hair and fastened around the base of his stem.

Despite his apprehension, a rush of blood made his balls pulse and his length harden.

He rolled his eyes as he groaned, willing himself not to respond to her, but unable to help it.

'What a beautiful boy you are,' cooed Amber, her fingers tickling the underside of his cock. 'What's it. Come out of your lair. Stand up and see what I have for you.'

Such was the allure in her voice, and such was Errol's own curiosity, that a second rush of blood sent a fresh stiffness rushing down his stem.

'Even better,' Amber breathed, her eyes widening as Errol's cock leapt into her hand. 'Pierre!'

Her order was sudden.

Pierre handed her something with his free hand.

Errol attempted to look down and see what Amber was doing. It wasn't easy. All he could see were some bits of loose leather.

But what he felt was enough to tell him exactly what she was doing.

Treacherous as it was, his penis swelled fit to burst as strips of leather were fastened along its length.

Panic would have taken him over, but the sensations emanating from his cock overwhelmed it. His body shook. Sweat trickled down his naked flesh as Amber gathered his balls in some kind of leather pouch.

A thin strap was passed between his buttocks. Another from the front of the harness. Both were buckled to a belt that Pierre fastened around his waist.

A smiling Amber stood upright and brought her face close to his.

'You're wearing a cock harness,' she said, her teeth hardly parting as she said it.

Errol stared at her as he fought to take in what she'd just said.

Amber raised her fine, plucked eyebrows.

'Aren't you going to thank me for it? No? Perhaps it's because it is not tight enough. You would like it tighter wouldn't you? Yes. I can see from your eyes you would like it tighter.'

Errol winced. He groaned, and his body stretched like a

string on a bow as Amber tightened the front buckle and Pierre did the one at the back.

'There', she purred, her hand running over his right buttock as she surveyed her handiwork. 'I do so like to see a cock enslaved to me.'

She raised her eyes to his.

'This,' she murmured, her fingers tapping on his still erect penis, 'is how I like to control the men who work for me.'

Sweat pouring down his face, Errol watched as Amber attached a red leather dog leash to the harness that held his cock.

Perennial smile still fixed on her face, she gave a sharp tug on the leash.

Errol's cry was muffled by the leather gag across his mouth. His hips were so far forward that he had no choice except to stand on tiptoe.

'This,' growled Amber in a crueller voice than before, 'is how it is done. So easy don't you think?'

Errol did not and could not answer. But he knew that she was right. Whatever she wanted him to do, he would have to do until such time as he could escape.

How he wished he had gone straight to New Orleans. If he had, he might have found Shirley Anne by now.

His penis, so tightly confined in the leather harness, pulsed both with pleasure and with pain. Amber laughed each time she tugged on it. Each time she let it go, she caressed the stretched muscles of his chest, his arched back, or his glistening buttocks.

He was in her power, totally subservient to whatever demands she made on him. Helpless, but not entirely unhappy.

However long it took, he would escape once the opportunity arose. To do that, he realised he must gain her trust, make her think he was as besotted with her as Pierre undoubtedly was. In order to fool her into thinking that, he must appear to enjoy whatever she did to him.

Think of Shirley Anne. Think of her every time she touches you.

Thinking of his wayward love sent his cock pulsing just as Amber yanked at it yet again.

He heard her cry with delight, saw her eyes widen with joy. He also saw the jealousy in the eyes of the silent Pierre and knew he had made an enemy.

Chapter 9

There was a party going on at the Catnip Club. A gay young thing was celebrating her twenty-first birthday and was out with all her friends, but none of the older members of her family.

She was dressed in a pretty pink dress with a large sash bound around her slim hips and a similar arrangement around her head.

Like her, her friends were dressed in light fabrics and bright colours, their faces aglow with all the energy and enthusiasm of youth. Fluttering and colourful, they flitted among their male companions, each movement of limb, each flickering of eyelid intended to entice.

'Give us more Ragtime, Maxie boy!' shouted a male member of her entourage. For some reason, this was the only man in her party who was not wearing a tuxedo, but white baggies, striped blazer, and a straw boater that sat too low over his eyes to be called natty.

Max, who hated being called Maxie, leaned low from the bandstand, put his lips to his horn, the end of the trumpet just inches from straw boater's face.

The trumpet screamed like a rogue bull elephant, the

blast sending straw boater a step backwards. By the time 'Jungle Jaunt Jam' was thudding through the club, all the young people were up and dancing, cheeks together, hand gripping partner's hand, and legs flying.

The music was taking them, making them dance like wooden marionettes, and it was Max making them do it.

Max himself was flying with the music. Once that aching, raunchy sound came out of his horn, he was no longer in the Catnip Club, but going with it as he would a train or a bus; like travelling, though not really going anywhere.

As he soared with the music, he thought of Emmeline and wondered how she was getting on without him. It was only when he played his horn that he was really with her again. Of course, he could go there for real if he liked, but Rene had hold of his contract, and Stacey kept hold of something else in order to make him stay.

Rene and Stacey knew as much about playing people as he did about playing horn. Of course, he and Emmeline had both known they were getting in deep with their sexual games, but life was for living wasn't it?

Neither had guessed that Rene had literally sold Emmeline's contract on to the guy from New York. That had been a year ago, and the contract was for a year. At least, that was what he had told Max.

He'd protested at first, but Stacey had promised to keep him sweet whilst his darling Emmeline was away. So far, she'd kept her promise.

He and Emmeline used to enjoy going out to the beach huts after the club was closed. As he pursed his lips and closed his eyes, his trumpet screamed and he remembered how the air blowing in from the sea had felt on their naked flesh. And how sleek and sexy Emmeline had looked with nothing but the light of the moon and the reflection from the water dancing over her body.

And she had danced there just for him, long legs kicking high above her head so that her sex thrust forward, the pinkness of her flesh glistening from between her dark-haired lips.

Stacey did her best to emanate what he and Emmeline used to do, but only what they did in the hut. She couldn't possibly try and be her entirely. For a start she couldn't dance, and secondly her flesh was too pale, her eyes blue, and her hair yellow as straw.

Little moonlight filtered into the crumbling beach hut, and if he narrowed his eyes, he could almost believe it was Emmeline he was with.

Stacey's breasts were as full and firm as Emmeline's, and her waist was just as narrow. She even had a belly that swelled just a little above her navel. Only when his fingers tangled into her pubic hair was the pretence slightly muted. Emmeline's pubic hair had a certain kind of wiry strength in it even though it felt silky. But Stacey's blonde, pubic curls were very soft. Very fine. Like the down on a dandelion, and fragile enough to be blown away.

He closed his eyes as the last strains of Sheree's number hit the high notes, then fell away to something like the growling purr of a mountain lion.

It was late by the time he blew the last blast on his horn. He saw Stacey over at the bar and could tell just by the way she was standing that she was expecting some action tonight. Well she wouldn't be getting it from him. He patted his breast pocket and heard the telegram rustle reassuringly. The year was almost up, and neither Rene or Stacey seemed unduly aware of it. So what? Who cares? As long as he knew she was coming back. Just occasionally, he wondered if they'd been entirely truthful. Was the contract really for a year? Or was it longer? He put the doubts from his mind. They were too difficult to live with.

After wiping the sweat from his brow, he made a big production of putting his horn away and accompanying Ted, one of his boys, a gangling type who played the trombone. He could almost feel Stacey's eyes boring into his back as he made his way out of the club.

'I'll be saying goodnight,' he said to Ted.

Ted stopped, his expression open and friendly. 'You're welcome to join me and a few of the boys for a party. We've even got some broads joining us – sisters or relatives of Chas I think.'

Max raised his eyebrows. 'More sisters? That mother of Chas must have had a daughter for every year of her life – including the year Chas was born!'

Ted laughed, his white teeth flashing in the darkness. 'Can't say Chas ever mentioned being a twin.'

'Can't say Chas ever mentioned having a sister before!'

Keeping to the shadows, Max made his way to an alley entrance that would take him home. Normally, he would take a taxi, but the stars were out and the air was warm. Besides, he was feeling good. Emmeline was coming home.

Checking that the coast was clear, he glanced along to where Rene and Stacey usually parked their car. Stacey was already in the car waiting.

Max was just about to turn into the alley, when he heard

the sound of the stage door closing. It was quickly followed by the recurrent click of a woman's shoes walking quickly along the sidewalk.

He stopped, turned, and immediately recognised the sleek figure of the new chanteuse, Sheree.

She started, then smiled when she saw it was him. He noticed her face was flushed and her eyes shining. Her smile made him feel almost as good as the telegram in his pocket.

'You walking tonight?' he asked.

She nodded.

'Yes. Stacey and Rene offered me a lift, but I told them I had a yearning to walk home tonight.'

Max nodded sagely as she fell in alongside him.

'It's a lovely night. A good night to walk home.' He took a deep breath.

'Is that magnolia I can smell, or is it your perfume.'

She laughed. 'I don't think any mere perfume can outshine the scent of magnolia. Do you?'

'Sometimes,' he answered, and smiled sadly.

Sheree, aware she had touched a raw nerve, looked down at her feet as she walked. She could feel that Max was missing someone. Probably because she was missing someone too.

Three months had gone since she had left home and, although she was still smitten with city life, there was an odd tickle under her heart that wouldn't go away.

Max stared straight ahead. He was feeling very aware of Sheree's presence. Although she might not know it, she definitely had something in common with his Emmeline. He made a great effort to keep things under control.

'I understand you've got the apartment in the Brabonne building.'

He said it as nonchalantly as he could, but it was hard not to infer some sense of misgiving.

Sheree did not answer straightaway. That in itself was enough to make Max hold his breath as he waited for her to speak. Of course he already knew she lived there. He just wanted to hear her say so. Wanted to know if she had found out Rene and Stacey's true natures.

'Yes. I do.'

'It's a nice place.'

'A lovely place. I've never lived in a place like it before.'

I bet you haven't, Max thought to himself.

Emmeline came into his thoughts again. Not that she often left them. But he knew what had happened there and perceived from Sheree's voice that something similar might have happened to her too. Suddenly, perhaps because Emmeline was on her way home, he felt excited, and feeling like that made him want to know more.

'Look . . .' he began, then hesitated. He sensed her looking at him as they walked, but only glanced at her then turned away, stunned by the green sparkle in her eyes, the gleaming black hair that framed her face like a tight-fitting hat, and the pink opulence of her lips.

'I wondered whether you've got time for a nightcap. I could walk you back to your place afterwards. No problem.'

He looked at her then. Saw her nod.

'Sure.' She smiled. 'Why not?'

He kept bourbon on a regular basis in the blue painted cupboard that had once graced the dispensing room of a long gone drug store. Emmeline had painted large treble clefts in gold paint on the front of it. 'To make it look as though you keep your horn in there,' she'd told him. Sure enough he did keep his trumpet in there. He kept the bourbon in there too plus a bottle of Emmeline's favourite wine.

'Bourbon?' he asked hopefully, unwilling to open the bottle he'd bought specially for Emmeline's homecoming.

Sheree nodded.

'A small one.'

Max raised his eyebrows as he threw her a questioning look.

Taking his meaning, Sheree smiled. 'OK. A large one. Hell, I've earned it.'

Max indicated a fat leather settee he'd rescued from some other place. It was old-fashioned but a helluva lot more comfortable than some of the mean bits of furniture being made nowadays.

Their fingers touched as the glass changed hands and Max's big heart leapt a beat when he heard the rasp of stocking against stocking as she crossed one slim leg over the other.

Nice legs, he thought to himself after the briefest of glances. He took a large swig of the bourbon, then another. Enough of the liquid was gone to warrant another.

'So,' he began once the burn of the liquid had eased in his throat. 'What made you come to New Orleans?'

Sheree took a decent slug from her glass. Then she leaned forward, slim elbows resting on one exposed knee.

'I wanted excitement. I wanted to taste the kind of life that I'd remember when my body and my stockings get wrinkled.'

Max laughed. 'I can never imagine you that way.'

Perhaps it was the whisky, or perhaps it was just her laugh and his excitement that Emmeline was coming home, but he was fast warming to her.

'Oh, I will be one day.' Sheree's eyes sparkled. 'But just once in my life I wanted to taste some glamour. Something different.'

Max nodded slowly. His glass was empty again and he was beginning to feel light-headed. Her glass still had some liquid in it, but little enough to constitute him asking if she wanted more.

She nodded and he filled both her glass and his.

They talked about where she came from, and where he came from. He talked about Emmeline. She talked about Errol.

'So why did she leave?'

Max was expecting the question, but did not welcome it. 'Well . . .' He took another slug of bourbon. It wasn't easy to think of what had happened, let alone talk about it. But his mind was floating and the bourbon had loosened his tongue.

'She had that same apartment you've got.' He paused again. This wasn't easy. 'It's a beautiful apartment. It's also a kind of . . .' It was hard to put it into words. He was also very aware that Sheree was staring quizzically at him, her brow furrowed. 'It's a kind of showcase,' he finished.

Sheree's frown deepened. 'Showcase? What does that mean?'

Suddenly, Max wished he hadn't said anything, but judging by the determination in her eyes, he wasn't going to get away with it now.

Max sighed. 'Rene tends to discover acts. Nurture them, you know, bring them on a bit. Once he thinks they're ready, he sells them on.'

'Sells them?'

Sheree's mouth had dropped open. Her lips were wet, partly because of the whisky.

Max shook his head. 'Not like that. Not like slaves. Pray God that doesn't happen any more around here. No. He gets them to sign their contract for a further year, then sells the contract on. Emmeline's in New York. At the Cotton Club.'

'Hey, you're not kidding!'

Sheree's eyes were suddenly bright with increased interest.

'Is he likely to do the same for me?'

Max eyed her finely chiselled face, the smooth skin and indescribable features. He judged that she wasn't quite as worldly wise as his beloved Emmeline, and if that was the case, he couldn't possibly tell her everything.

'Oh sure. He'll do it for you alright.'

'Wow!'

Max had been going to tell her about what went on at the place she was living, and also what went on at the old Brabonne mansion. But her brightness and the drink was affecting him. Suddenly, it all seemed of no consequence. Besides, the things that went on at both of those places only served to strengthen the desire he was feeling in his loins.

Sheree's expression was one of breathless anticipation. Her eyes were fixed on his and, because her mouth was open slightly, her moist lips seemed to be inviting his own.

He didn't quite know how he came to be lying on the settee beside her. All he knew was she smelt good and was now only dressed in a soft silk camisole top and lace-edged French knickers. There was a lovely expanse of naked flesh between her knickers and her stocking tops. Exposure, he thought, was a funny thing. Just that bit of flesh showing made her seem more naked than if she were wearing nothing at all.

He'd taken off his jacket. His tie was gone. His shirt undone. *Hell, I don't remember doing that*, he thought.

'Should we be doing this?' Her voice and her breath was soft and warm against his ear.

'It's part of our nature.' He kissed her. 'It's part of our artistic nature.'

She murmured and arched herself closer to him as his hands ran down over her back and curved over her behind. Firm, he thought to himself. And such a lovely shape. Round, and the two halves segregated by a deep cleft that gave them a sort of individuality.

As he kissed her, he pulled the silk of her French knickers up over her behind, then gathered it into her cleft so that only the sisterly orbs were left exposed.

Max closed his eyes as his fingers kneaded the firm flesh. He brought one hand over her hips and let it slide down between them. Again, he slid the silk of her knickers to one side. His fingers met the silky luxuriance of her pubic hair, and the feel of it made him sigh and forget himself.

'Emmeline,' he whispered.

'Emmeline?'

'I'm sorry.'

They paused. She looked into his eyes, her fingers caressing the nape of his neck.

'It doesn't matter. In fact, I think it's a very good idea. I can be Emmeline until she gets back. You can be Errol.'

Max nodded silently. 'Yes,' he murmured before his lips again sought hers.

Max felt the surge of blood pulse into his penis as he slid his hands up under the pretty peach camisole. Her ribcage was smooth and lean enough, but the feel of her breasts beneath his hands occasioned the biggest erection he'd ever had. It throbbed against his trouser buttons and his sighs of passion almost turned to a sigh of relief as Sheree began unbuttoning his trousers.

Her breasts seemed to thrust against his hands and the firm prettiness of them was almost enough to take his breath away.

He groaned as his thumb flicked over her hard, tight nipples. A delicious feeling of triumph seemed to curl down his spine and make his pelvis thrust forward as her nipples grew.

One hand still playing with her rear, he pulled the camisole top up, bent his head and took her nipple onto his tongue.

She arched her back and cried a small cry that told him she was in ecstasy. He sucked on her, nibbled the firm flesh, and took as much of her into his mouth as he could possibly manage.

This was no Stacey, he told himself. It wasn't even Emmeline. It was someone else. Sheree. Someone who he seemed completely in tune with – at least – for the moment.

Blood racing, he chose to think that he wouldn't be long in coming. Giddy with lust, he forced himself to carefully consider exactly how he wanted to finish this. Max let his mind drift back to the very first time with Emmeline on this very settee.

It had been Emmeline's idea to christen it. The man they bought it from was in the front office when they did it, but the hint of danger only added to the excitement.

Emmeline had knelt on the settee, hands and chin resting on its back. Hardly believing his luck and the sheer audacity of their intentions, Max had rolled her skirt up over her back, then eased her underwear to one side.

First, he looked at the lush pink lips pouting through a fringe of coal-black hair. He'd touched it, felt its moistness and its warmth and, as he did so, his rod had grown, only attracting his attention when a button had popped off sounding like a thunderclap in the stillness.

Nothing could ever equal that sweet moment when his glans had nuzzled her pink flesh, then slid unopposed into the slippery moist aperture that bid him welcome.

Thumb hooked in knickers, he held them to one side so he could more easily enjoy the look and the sight of her bare behind.

He had gripped her hips as his own pelvis had thudded backwards and forwards, the excitement of the moment heightened each time they saw a shadow move across the glass of the door that divided them from the front office.

As his moment came nearer, his hands went to her belly then down between her legs.

He heard her moan, felt the thrust of her bottom against him as she sought the pleasure his fingers could give her.

This was what was happening now, only it was Sheree who was crying out with pleasure, her sex wet with juice, her hips jerking against him as he thudded his essence into her.

As he lay over her back and, breathless, gently kissed her ear, he glanced briefly at the door, then smiled. They had climaxed in private.

What a difference, he thought with amusement. Back then, on that first time with Emmeline, the door opened at exactly the same time as they orgasmed.

The baptist minister had stood dumbstruck, his jaw looking like an elevator that had dropped three levels instead of one. Emmeline, a fallen Catholic, had seen the funny side of it.

'Bless me father, for I have sinned.'

Max smiled to himself. Emmeline was a born sinner, and she thoroughly enjoyed her birthright.

Chapter 10

Emmeline caught the ten ten at Grand Central. Unusually for someone taking such a long trip, she was looking forward to it. Her fellow passengers might well be as boring as the track-side scenery but, at the end, Max would be waiting for her. In between she would have to amuse herself and she was pretty good at doing that.

She eyed a few of her fellow passengers who sat like little islands in their seats, occupying themselves with tedious monotony, a thickly oppressive shield against the intrusion of some talkative fellow passenger.

There they all sat, some already in the process of knitting, reading, or just staring out of the window. One man was attempting to play a card game on a suitcase that was precariously balanced on his lap. She smiled at him. A startled pallor came to his face, a flurry of nervous blinking to his eyes before he went back to his cards.

No entertainment there, she told herself and sighed. This journey might feel like a lifetime.

They were three hours into the trip before her backside really began to make buttons.

'Excuse me,' she said to the middle-aged woman sat next to her.

The woman, who had seemed to be merely daydreaming, got huffily up, no doubt unhappy at being disturbed from something that might well have been more interesting than her life.

Emmeline decided an apology was in order. After all, this was liable to be a long journey and could seem even longer sat next to a miserable companion.

'Sorry, but I just have to stretch my legs.' She smiled sweetly. The woman gave her a quick smile and a cursory nod, but no words. Words were like opening the doors to the Bastille. Conversation might come pouring in.

Lilting gently from side to side with the motion of the car, Emmeline made her way the length of the train without seeing either a person who looked interesting, or who had the sort of expression that betrayed they were interested in her.

Eventually, Emmeline came to the far end of the train and faced the door that none are supposed to enter.

Glancing over her shoulder, she tried the handle without knocking and went in. The smell of leather was oddly welcoming. The voice that greeted her was not.

'What do you want?'

The luggage car was fairly gloomy, but good enough to see where the voice had come from.

The guard was probably in his early thirties, had a square jaw, blue eyes and a fair complexion. He was sitting on a suitcase which was lower than the large travelling chest that was serving as a table. A deck of playing cards was spread out in a game of Solitaire.

Anything Goes

Emmeline glanced at the cards, then looked straight at him. A feathery light kind of feeling filled her stomach. It was as if a heap of cotton boles had been blasted into the air in thousands of pieces and was floating on a breeze. Words seemed long in coming.

The guard spoke again.

'What can I do for you?'

His manner was not exactly polite about her intrusion into his domain, but it eased off a bit when he saw how well she was packaged.

'I'm like you,' she said.

The guard pushed his cap back further on his head. 'What?'

'I'm bored.' She smiled and trailed her fingers over the cards. 'Care for a different kind of game?'

Her smile widened. She rested her hands on the hips of her slim white suit, her pose leaving him in no doubt of what he could gain from such a game.

'Now,' she said as she slid a suitable suitcase over the opposite side of the luggage trunk from his and sat down. 'Let me explain the rules to you. This is called Strip Jack. You lose, you take an item of clothes off. I lose . . .' She smiled provocatively. 'Get the picture?'

Eyes wide with surprise, the guard nodded.

'Right.'

'What about . . .?' the guard swallowed hard before continuing. 'What about when we've got all our clothes off . . . when we're naked?'

Emmeline leaned closer to him. 'A good question. Let me explain. Once we're buck naked, we count up who's won the most games. Whoever comes out . . .' She paused again.

'On top . . .' she smiled. 'Gets to choose what we do next and how we do it. How's that grab you?'

The guard swallowed again. 'It grabs me.'

Emmeline was good at cards, but only when she wanted to be. She knew how to win, but she also knew how to lose. It depended what the stake was, and in this case it would please her to lose.

The guard groaned each time she removed a garment. When he lost his first game, he removed a shoe. When Emmeline lost her first game, she had slipped off her shoe and, making a big play of it, had run her hands up over her stocking and taken off her garter.

As the game wore on and she lost more hands and more clothes, her movements became more provocative, more arousing to the poor man who had thought he would be playing Solitaire all the way down south.

She held his gaze as she pulled her silk underwear up to her shoulders. He gasped when he saw the bells that hung from her breasts and she could imagine the furore the sight of them was causing in his pants. His eyes went back to them each time the bells tinkled to the movement of the train.

Even when she was down to just her shoes and her underwear, it was her knickers that went first.

She stood up as she slid them down her long, lean legs, smiling as the pink-faced guard gazed open mouthed at this woman who stood before him dressed in a pair of shoes and a pair of flesh-coloured silk stockings.

Of course, she lost the last two games too.

'You've won the most,' she said to the guard who stood naked too. 'What do you want and how do you want it?'

Anything Goes

Trembling, the man got to his feet. Emmeline's eyes raked his body, her tongue lightly licking her bottom lip as she imagined the feel of him; the taste of him.

Judging by the length and thickness of the instrument that thrust so proudly from a clutch of reddish pubic hair, it was pretty easy to see what the poor man wanted. It pulsated, seeming to thrust forward of its own accord, driven by a thought in its own mind. Milk white, a lozenge of liquid oozed trembling like an excited teardrop on its tip, a foretaste of the libation to come.

'How do you want it?' Emmeline asked again, her voice husky with a simmering lust that seemed to cover her body like a cobweb of silk.

The man licked at his lips as Emmeline did a slow twirl, her hands cupping her breasts as though presenting them as gifts to his gaze.

'This way?' she said, standing with legs apart, thrusting her hips forward so his eyes could see the delicate frills of flesh that furled like petals between her pubic lips. 'Or this way?'

Buttocks towards him, she bent over, her eyes studying his reaction over her shoulder. He barely seemed to notice her face, his gaze fixed firmly on the delight that was being so wantonly offered him.

To her great delight, she saw him blink, heard his sharp intake of breath, and saw his cock tremble.

Dragging his eyes away from her, his gaze went to the luggage trunk. The cards were still scattered over it. Thick straps bound it firmly shut.

Some unspoken message flashed between them. The luggage trunk was like a catalyst, a meeting point for like minds. Each of them interpreted what the other was thinking. Emmeline knew what he wanted, and she wanted it too.

Smiling, Emmeline draped herself over the trunk, her own flesh slightly lighter than its tan shininess.

'I think you'd like me like this, wouldn't you?'

The guard stammered.

'Wouldn't you?' Emmeline repeated. 'After all, you're stuck with this luggage for hours. Imagine. In future you could look at all this stuff in an entirely new way.'

Suddenly, eyes blazing with a kind of sexual madness, the guard sprang into life.

'You're right,' he cried. 'You're right!'

Just as she had hoped, he unbuckled the straps of the trunk, slid her wrists beneath them, then rebuckled them. In order for him to better appreciate her predicament, she wriggled her hands as if she were trying to escape. She saw his eyes gleam; knew she had done the right thing. Being bound to an object that dominated his working life had made her part of it. He wanted her to be part of it. Wanted to take out his frustration with his job on her. But he also wanted her to protest – just as if it were the luggage trunk protesting. But it couldn't escape. He was in charge now.

Flushed with excitement, he spread her knees over each opposite corner of the trunk and strapped her ankles around its base. His hands fumbled with the buckles, his breathing rushed and hot against her legs. Then, panting, he stood and looked at her.

His eyes stared. Perspiration glistened on his face and a nerve throbbed in his temple. He seemed overcome by some thought in his mind that no one else knew about.

I must look like some sacrifice, Emmeline thought, *and*

this man will remember me all his life. Each time he looks at a piece of luggage, he'll see more than brown leather, thick straps and buckles. He'll see me. He'll always see me.

She began to move her body, raising her hips, arching her back, writhing provocatively in an effort to entice him to take her. Those feathery feelings she had felt earlier were now fanning out all over her body. A light flush coloured her cheeks and an excited brightness lit her eyes. Soon he would take her. He had to take her.

So sure was she of her own allure and her confidence at always controlling events, that his next actions were totally unexpected.

He picked up a piece of coiled leather, unfurled it and began to walk around the trunk and her. Her eyes followed him, fixed on the leather.

'I hate luggage,' he muttered. 'I hate the way it fills my life. I'm sure there's better things could fill it. God, how I hate you!'

The air whistled as the strip of leather flew through it.

Emmeline gasped, then squeezed her eyes shut and cried out.

There was a loud crack. Emmeline opened her eyes. She felt no pain, so obviously the strip of leather had not hit her.

'I hate luggage!'

'You certainly do,' she murmured, hardly daring to raise her voice and bring his attention and his blows down on her.

The leather kissed the air a few more times and, each time the blow landed on the sides of the trunk to which she was tied and thankfully not on her body.

Strangely enough, she felt a kind of jealousy towards the trunk. It seemed silly, but why should it get more attention than her? She was also getting impatient to be mounted. After all, that's what she was after.

'What sort of man are you?' she cried out. 'Is that all you're fit for? To be a baggage-car attendant?'

The guard's eyes narrowed. His bottom lip shuddered and his cheeks reddened. 'You bitch! You're no better than this lot!'

Emmeline cringed. *He's crazy*, she thought. Then calmed herself once she judged it was the luggage he hated, not her.

All the same, her ill-chosen words had done their work. The leather sang in the air again, but this time it left a red stripe across her belly.

'No!' she cried out.

'Yes!' cried the guard.

The leather left another red stripe across her breasts, across her thighs. Each time the blow landed, she saw that the guard's penis throbbed and grew. She might yet get what she'd come here for and, despite her discomfort, her hungry eyes settled on his iron-hard erection.

At last he stood between her legs, his thighs braced, the muscles bulging as his whole body tensed. His stomach was tight, a line of hair running down its middle, connecting the fine hair of his chest with the golden-red forest that encircled his member.

He was a beautiful sight. A golden Adonis whose cock could plug the juicy crevice of her body and fill her belly with its silky warm ambrosia.

The sight of him, and the thought of how well he could fill her, were too much for the panting Emmeline. She wanted his cock and she wanted it now.

'Put it in!' she demanded, her legs straining against their

restraints, her breasts quivering in time with the rhythm of the train and the writhing of her body. 'Put it in!' she cried again.

She saw his eyes glittering. Saw his penis throbbing. His gaze was fixed on the thickly haired lips of her sex and the small bell that hung from her clitoris.

She gasped as he flicked at it with the leather which he had now folded in two. The bell tinkled and her clitoris throbbed excitedly.

He was like a small boy who has just discovered the greatest toy ever. He did it again and she moaned.

Suddenly, it occurred to her that spending all his time being locked up with other people's baggage might well have turned the guard's mind and made him completely crazy. More frightened now, she began to struggle.

He laughed.

'It's no good. You won't loose them straps. Good quality, they are. Best money can buy.'

His laugh now seemed no different than the tone of his voice. It was as if the luggage car and the jolting train no longer existed. Whatever he was seeing, it wasn't necessarily her or the luggage.

'Just like this,' he said whilst waving the folded strip of leather. 'Just like this,' he murmured again as he flicked the leather at the bell and then at her exposed flesh.

Each time his blow landed, a tingling vibration seared through Emmeline's clitoris, trembled through her pubic lips, and spread all over her body like a series of mild electric shocks.

'Don't do that,' she whimpered as she felt the leather being pushed into her body. 'Please . . .'

Her voice faded into a low, shameful moan. It wasn't his prick going into her. It was a piece of leather and, because his thumb was playing with her clitoral bell, she was enjoying it. Her muscles were easing aside to welcome the intruder. The word 'hussy' raced around her mind. But she couldn't help it. He was doing the right things, at the right tempo with the wrong object. But it wasn't really wrong. It was stiff and, at the same time, it was soft.

Despite the vulnerability of her position, she could not help moaning with pleasure, writhing against her bonds, her bottom rising off the cold leather of the trunk as the guard worked the leather into her.

'Stop doing that!'

'What?'

She didn't understand what the guard was talking about, but she groaned regretfully when he left the leather hanging from her, rummaged in some hidden closet, and came back with a thicker strap made of the same sort of webbing they use for saddle girths.

'This'll keep you still, girl!'

He growled as he said it, the stiff coarseness of the strap rough against her nipples as he ran it across her breasts and tightened it at each side.

Now, it was almost impossible to move and her breasts were flattened against her ribs, her nipples brazenly swollen against the coarseness of the fabric and the hard metal bells that adorned them.

She moaned, not at the way her breasts were being abused, but because she wanted the guard to carry on with what he was doing.

He did. 'Now don't move,' he ordered. 'Just moan.'

As he resumed the tempo he had temporarily abandoned, she did just that.

She was aware that her juice was now in full flow, probably trickling down the side of the luggage trunk. The small bell on her clitoris was ringing crazily and her breasts felt like two windblown fruit.

Sensing that the guard was using her as a surrogate suitcase, she groaned her climax rather than shouting out with joy.

The sound seemed to please him. As she lay like a damp rag doll, he pulled the leather out and – how, she didn't really know – he turned her over, adjusting her bonds slightly to make the task easier.

'Up a bit,' she heard him say, and even before he did it, she knew he was going to push a smaller suitcase under her hips so that her bottom stuck up that much more than the rest of her.

Instinctively, she knew what would come first. She tensed, preparing her soft flesh for the ritual abuse to come.

First, she felt the strip of leather across her bottom, its bite leaving a fiery heat in its wake. She yelped, her breasts crushed now against the luggage trunk, her decorative bells digging into her flesh.

Again and again the leather rose and fell and with each stroke, her bottom became hotter until it felt like flesh roasted before the dying embers of a red-hot fire.

Then he stopped.

'Nice and pink,' he said. 'Like pigskin.'

The sound of his voice made her shiver. She wanted to say something, but bit her lip. No matter what she thought of saying, all of it seemed oddly provocative, an encouragement for him to do to her as he pleased.

Even though his palms were warm, a chillness ran over her flesh as he fondled each buttock. He was muttering to himself; odd words, odd noises. None of what he was saying was for her.

His hands continued to caress her behind, to push her stinging spheres together. To pull them apart so that she felt a coldness between them and the shame of exposure.

'I don't believe it,' she whispered as one finger slid between her buttocks. 'The dirty swine!' she added as its tip nudged at the small hole hidden there.

'Nice and warm,' he said again. 'Almost ready.'

His hands left her. Just as she had expected, she felt the sting of the leather.

She cried out with each blow, just as he wanted her to. After all, he was taking revenge out on luggage in general, and she was his go between.

Her flesh burned but, at the same time, her sex felt heavy with the need to finish this.

After about ten strokes, he stopped. She trembled beneath his touch, her voice a low, grateful moan, for the hands that rubbed her buttocks seemed so cool in comparison with her own flesh.

'Lovely,' he murmured. 'That'll keep me warm.'

Suddenly, he was close between her thighs, his penis nudging between the cheeks of her behind before travelling lower, the slickness of his glans easily entering her body.

She tensed as his whole length pushed into her, but then relaxed as he began to thrust backwards and forwards, her muscles gripping his length as if unwilling to let him go.

He murmured about how warm her bottom was against his groin, then he lay flat on her so that her breasts, and indeed her whole body, were squashed against the luggage trunk.

The thrust of his loins was fast and furious. It was as though it was the trunk he was fucking and not a woman at all. But, despite the fact that she had only recently climaxed, her sex was getting wet again. She hadn't meant to get into this situation, but now she was in it, she was damn well going to enjoy it.

Soon she became lost in the ecstasy of it all and, because of that, she began to murmur instead of moan. The guard heard her.

'I'm not making myself plain!' he exclaimed.

She caught her breath as he withdrew. Suddenly, she knew what was coming next.

He held the cheeks of her bottom apart between finger and thumb.

Emmeline tensed, sure of what was going to happen.

She was right. She felt her own wetness and the hardness of his glans press against her smallest hole. She tried to use her muscles to block him out, but he was too forceful.

'This is my revenge!'

Her anus filled up with his stiffness, muscles bending, folding apart from the onslaught of his penis.

Emmeline cried out as he buried himself in her, rubbing his groin against the heat of her bottom, then lying full length on her again so that her breasts were tightly squashed whilst her behind was being abused.

But her own enjoyment was not entirely obliterated. The little bell that hung from her clitoris was exerting its own pressure.

Although her cries sounded anguished, there was a low tremor of pleasure reverberating through them.

The guard cried out like a triumphant general who's just won his most important battle. His fluid gushed into her and, as she felt its heat fill her back passage, she cried out herself and did her best to make it sound full of pain rather than pleasure.

She felt no shame afterwards. How else can a captive survive?

Chapter 11

Errol moved forward on his knees in response to his mistress tugging on the leather and metal harness that encircled his balls and his stem. It wasn't too uncomfortable. In fact, it wasn't dissimilar to the pulling hand of an enthusiastic woman.

'You've learned well,' Amber purred. 'Come closer.'

He made his way forward on bended knees, the thickness of a Persian carpet beneath him.

Amber was lying full stretch on her favourite lounger, her flaming hair tumbling like molten fire over her shoulders. Her eyes gleamed with a mix of power and lust.

Errol glanced at her, and his penis stiffened. Amber had been made by Mother Nature for one thing only, and she'd never rebuked Mother Nature for doing so.

Her breasts rose steeply with each lustful breath. Her nipples peeped through the gap in her silk robe which lazed halfway down her arms and barely covered the voluptuous curves of her body.

Errol was naked, his well-developed muscles glistening from the oil Pierre had rubbed into them, his flesh warm with a blood supply encouraged by the manservant's probing fingers.

At first he had not liked Pierre touching his flesh in such a familiar fashion. Another man's fingers exploring his body had made him feel strange. But there was no sexual motive behind his actions. Pierre explained that he was preparing him exactly as his mistress liked her man-things prepared. He would please her, and that was all that mattered.

Gradually, despite the fact that he was securely chained to a bench throughout, Errol had become adjusted to Pierre's ministrations. He reasoned that if he could gain both Pierre's and his mistress's confidence, he might be released from his chains. Once freed from those, it would be easy to escape.

Again he felt the tug on the harness which pulled his balls and penis forward begging his body to follow.

Dutifully, he shuffled forward and, as Pierre had instructed him, kept his eyes downcast until ordered otherwise.

He still wore the thick leather collar he had worn that first day and the leather patch across his mouth. His arms were behind his back, his wrists fastened to a link at the back of his collar. His ankles were hobbled together. If he got up, he could walk, but only slowly. Impossible if he wanted to run.

The harness that fastened around his waist also wound up between his buttocks. At first he had wondered about the strange feeling between them, but was told later on that he wore an anal plug.

'It is so you can feel what it is like to have your body

invaded – just like a woman does.'

That was what Pierre had told him.

Amber pulled him a bit closer again and laughed lightly as she tapped one finger on the end of his penis.

What a traitor, Errol thought as, despite its entrapment, his tool leapt boldly towards her hand. Inwardly, Errol groaned. One touch and it leapt from his body.

'I see you are on form. As usual.'

Amber smiled and Errol felt pleased. Something in her deep green eyes betrayed the fact that she was besotted with him. Perhaps responding to her sexual advances so quickly and so well would be the key to his escape. With that in mind, he let his sexuality run free.

The musky smell of her pussy drifted over his face as she opened her legs.

He drank in her smell and, as he did so, he felt his groin contract and his penis expand. What use for other aphrodisiacs compared to the scent of a woman?

Her smile was languid. So was the way she lay full stretch on the lounger, her silk robe whispering as it slid further down her arms.

A long case clock with a brass face struck midday.

'Lunch time,' said Amber, her green eyes smiling along with her red lips. Her long fingers unfastened the buckle that held his mouth restraint in place. It fell free to swing beneath his chin. His jaw dropped too and he took a deep breath.

Amber smiled knowingly and her fingers caressed his cheek. 'Eat your lunch, slave.'

He could have said something at that point. Could have refused or at least made some trivial comment. But he knew better than that. He'd done that once before and she had got very angry, told him it was not his place to say anything. He was her sex slave. A creature who existed purely to service her body and be played with in any manner she wished.

Her punishment on that occasion was still in his mind.

She had ordered Pierre to chain him against the wall, arms high above his head. Then she had done the most abominable thing possible.

Tightly chained and unable to cry out because the gag had been replaced, Errol had watched as Pierre had strapped a rubber penis around his mistress.

All the time he was doing this, Amber stood perfectly still, her eyes glittering, her mouth set in a firm line as she glared at him.

'A punishment any man would prefer to avoid,' she said, her mouth twisting in a cruel grin. 'Pierre!'

Out of the corner of his eye, Errol saw Pierre open a white jar on the table, dip into it, and take some of its creamy contents onto his fingers.

A mix of terror and revulsion had raced through his body as Pierre applied the cold cream between Errol's buttocks.

Then Amber came close, her perfume intoxicating and the touch of her fingers arousing despite the precariousness of his position.

Resting her cheek against his shoulder blade, she wrapped herself around him. For the first time ever, Errol felt a stiff penis – albeit a false one – nudge between his buttocks.

He squeezed his eyes shut and a harsh cry ripped through his mind as Amber pushed the stiff rod into his body. A stiffness permeated his muscles. This, he told himself, would be a torture that was almost impossible to endure. His mind screamed. His anus burned with the fierceness of her intrusion. He writhed his tormented body, intent on making things as difficult for her as possible, but it didn't last.

Just at the point where he was about to put as much strength as possible into throwing her off his back, her hands ran down over his belly. Relaxation came to his muscles, but a new stiffness came to his penis.

Slowly, she began to move her pelvis. As the penis moved in and out of him, her fingers began to pull on his penis and, shame of shames, he began to enjoy what she was doing to him.

Due to the ministrations of her hands and the sheer decadence of what she was doing to him, his seed rushed up his shaft and spilt onto the ground.

His body trembled with the onslaught of it, the warm fluid splashing against the stone wall and trickling down the front of his legs.

It should have stopped there, but it didn't. That was the torture of it.

'Just because you have finished with my hands, doesn't mean I've finished with you,' Amber said.

The torture went on. Why shouldn't it? Amber could go on for hours if she wanted. Her erection would never die because it wasn't real.

But the discomfort was, and Errol had no intention of repeating it. And this time he had every intention of avoiding it.

Still on his knees, Errol took one step, then bent his head, eyeing the luxuriance of her pubic foliage before her moistness covered his face like a warm mist rising from still water.

Her pubic lips seemed to part of their own accord as his tongue slid between them. Her clitoris seemed to leap into his mouth, swollen and hot like a heavily erected penis.

The flesh of her inner thighs shone whitely on either side of his face and, as he did luscious things to her flesh, she hummed an inconsequential tune and sighed when his tongue worked its way into her vagina.

Being a passionate man, Errol was not unaffected by the smell of her, the feel of her hot flesh against his mouth. His penis, still tightly constrained by the cock harness, felt large enough to burst. It ached with lust, its hardness pulsating with pent-up fluid that gathered like a tidal wave behind its fragile ramparts.

He took a breath, raised his head and glanced briefly at the woman whose sex he was almost eating.

The whiteness of her breasts rose like twin peaks of the High Sierra above him. Her head was thrown back. Her eyes were closed, but her mouth was open.

The tune she was humming and her sighs were now one and the same, an odd musical cacophony of sensual sounds that ably expressed exactly what she was feeling.

As he watched her, he took long licks of her pubic hair, tasting her saltiness and slicking the hair flat against her flesh.

Trancelike, she lay there, her body exposed and open to him. Her mind, he decided, was enraptured by the sensations it was receiving from that part of a woman's body that is made to be fucked.

And it shall be, he suddenly decided. *It definitely shall be!*

Licking up over her belly, he eased himself onto his feet, his body sliding up over her behind his tongue. His mouth lingered on the ripe breasts of his mistress, his teeth and tongue sucking and biting at her nipples until they rose like two shining, red rosebuds from the whiteness of a field of lilies.

Her eyes flickered, then opened as his face came close to hers.

Errol halted. Would she protest? Would he again have to suffer the indignity of a woman fucking him?

'What do you want, Errol?' she asked.

Errol swallowed. He had to sound convincing. 'You,' he said softly, provocatively. 'I want you. I want to make love to you.'

Amber blinked, and for a moment a tremor of fear ran through Errol's body.

Then she smiled, and he knew he was saved. He had said the right words. He hadn't used the more vulgar terminology. He had used the words of a man intent on seducing a beautiful woman on her terms, not those of a man.

There was a stillness between them for a moment. Errol was aware that his penis was throbbing and moistening no more than half an inch from her sex. He was also aware that she was staring at him as though seeing a man for the first time in her life.

'Why do you want to make love to me, Errol?'

Errol gathered all the confidence he could. What and how he said this would count for everything.

'Because you're beautiful. In fact, I think you're the most

beautiful, the most sexually adventurous woman I have ever met in my whole life.'

Amber stared, her eyes wide, her features stiff like some wax effigy confined to a glass case in a Catholic church.

Then she smiled and her features softened.

'Then do it to me,' she said.

Holding himself just right, Errol pushed into her. He didn't lunge at her as though his prick was a battering ram, but took it slowly, carefully, as though she were a virgin and each inch was a step through initial pain rather than lasting pleasure.

Because his hands were still fastened to the thick leather collar that encircled his throat, he could not touch her breasts. He could only rub his chest against them, revelling in them as if they were feather cushions flung there for him to enjoy. In return, each nipple thrust like two hard peas against his chest.

Despite Amber being sexually adventurous, this was the first time Errol had actually performed for her in this manner.

Up until this moment, Amber had taken him whenever she wanted, her riding him, sitting on his prick, bouncing on him as she might some horse she was riding.

Once she had come, she would dismount leaving him stiff and unsatisfied.

'Learn to come at the same time I do if you want satisfaction,' she had told him.

He had heeded her words. On the odd occasion afterwards when he hadn't done that, Amber had taken great delight in having Pierre finish him by hand whilst she looked on, smiling – always smiling.

Chapter 12

'I have a special request, *ma chérie*,' whispered Rene against Sheree's nearly cut bob.

Sheree's skin tingled as though a fine electric charge had brushed against her. It reminded her of being out in a storm when the thunderheads are dark and the rain oddly piercing before the thunder sounds and the lightning flashes through the clouds.

He's married to Stacey. That was the thought that went through her mind. So what? It didn't seem to matter to Stacey. It didn't seem to matter much to Rene either.

Her painted lips parted as she turned to look at him.

'What do you want me to do?'

Rene smiled, his dark moustache seeming to stretch across his face and the familiar creases appearing at the sides of his eyes.

She held her breath as he kissed her cheek, her throat, then the nape of her neck.

'I want you to go on stage tonight without wearing any underwear.'

She gasped. Once she'd taken the request in, she looked at him wide-eyed.

Her lips formed a word, but no sound came out.

'You seem surprised. So I will ask you again. For me, my darling Sheree. Go onto that stage wearing that beautiful pale mauve dress I've just bought you. Wear that, and nothing else. Nothing.'

Sheree's thoughts went to the slinky mauve dress that fitted her like a second skin.

Stacey had been with her when she bought it. The money, Stacey had told her, was courtesy of the Catnip Club, and Rene, its patron, in particular.

'Don't you think it's a bit tight?' she'd said.

Stacey had leaned against the changing-room door, her eyelids and sockets seeming twice the expanse they were because her eyebrows were plucked so severely.

'Without the underwear, it will be fine. Try it.'

Sheree had looked at herself in the mirror. Telltale grooves in the material outlined the waistband of her knickers and top.

'I do have some more close-fitting underwear at home,' she murmured, her heart thudding because Stacey was watching her so intently.

'So you have it at home, sweetness. But that isn't here is it. Take off your underwear and you can see the damn frock at its best. Come here. I'll help you.'

Without waiting for Sheree to reply, Stacey lay her cigarette holder in an ashtray.

She peeled the dress away from Sheree's body as though she were skinning an orange or a line. Once it was down at her ankles, Stacey's fingers went to the waistband of Sheree's knickers. Sheree herself pulled her cami-top off over her head. By the time she was free of it, Stacey's hands were guiding her knickers down past Sheree's knees and her cheek was resting casually against her bottom.

'There,' Stacey said with a hint of triumph, a bemused smile playing around her lips as she regarded Sheree's flushed face via the mirror. 'See? No lumps!'

As she said it, she ran her hands over Sheree's hips, stroking her as if she were some shy, wild fawn about to flee to lonely places.

'Now try it without the underwear,' Stacey suggested.

Helped by her boss's wife, Sheree slid the soft, gauzy fabric back up over her body.

Pink-faced, she stared at her reflection, aware that Stacey, who was fastening the dress at the back, was also staring.

'You look provocative,' Stacey had breathed, her chin resting on Sheree's shoulder. 'You look as though you could have any man in the room, and any man in the room could have you.'

Sheree had not replied. She had just stared at the two spots where her nipples pushed against the fabric, areolae easily seen.

In the deep vee between her legs, she could see a dark triangular shadow.

Stacey was right. She did look provocative.

'Will you do it for me?'

Rene's voice brought Sheree back to the present. As he said it, he passed her a glass of something purple that was decorated with black and green olives.

Sheree trembled at the touch of his fingers; looked into his eyes as she sipped her bitter-sweet drink.

The spirit rushed straight to her head. Or was it desire?

'Yes,' she said throatily, the liquid glistening on her lips. 'Yes. I will do it for you.'

He made no attempt to leave her dressing room. He merely leaned against the door jamb, smoking and watching through a thick blue haze of cigar smoke, his face quiet, his eyes dancing.

The dress, she realised, was indeed of too fine a fabric to wear with any sort of underwear, even her most translucent.

Before Rene's very eyes, she disrobed, aware as she did so that her employer was scrutinising every inch of her body, his eyes caressing her in a parody of affectionate hands.

She averted her eyes as she took off her flimsy undergarments, unwilling to look at him and feel herself blushing as she did so. It was almost as if she were afraid he might see the excitement in her eyes. It was also to do with the desire she would see in his.

'Beautiful,' he said, his hand following the curve of her spine once she was dressed again and heading for the stage and her public. 'Like a sleek, sensual python.'

Maybe it was him saying that, or maybe it was the feel of the fragile fabric against her skin, but when she sang, her body swayed. Her flesh tingled.

She was aware of Max looking at her. She was also aware that every man in the audience was licking his lips. It was as though each one was imagining the feel of her nipple between his teeth, or the taste of her pussy on his tongue.

> 'Make me your night-time baby,
> Make me your midday love.
> Don't give me your sometime, maybe,
> Give me your full-time love.'

As she sang, she ran her hands over her body, tracing her sweeping curves, cupping the firm pertness of her breasts, the pink nipples staring like rosebud eyes at the audience.

Music drifted from her mouth and her very presence seemed to drift away with it.

She was soaring, flying away from the club and from New Orleans. Nothing bound her either to the earth, or to a man. She was a free spirit when she sang and sometimes it seemed she was floating out among the audience, overhearing things she shouldn't be hearing, peering into people's minds and seeing things that no one else could see.

Her spirit soared. Rene was nearby. In his mind she could see herself naked, and Rene ravishing her.

She also picked up a scene in Stacey's mind. Stacey was standing, watching what her husband was doing. Sheree strained to see what she was looking at. Her voice shook. Her body trembled. She had seen herself.

As the last notes soared to the ceiling, the sunshine brightness of the spotlight fell on her body.

Its sudden attention made her freeze for the briefest of moments. Then she smiled, threw up her arms and stood with legs apart.

A hushed gasp went up from the audience. Then applause. Loud, stupendous, ear-splitting applause that fell like cracked sticks from people's palms and, at the same time, cries of endeavour, of encouragement, and even of affection, exploded in the audience.

The band behind her joined in. Sheree threw everyone kisses, aware that she had sung well, but not entirely sure that it was her singing and only her singing that had attracted that sort of attention.

It was Max who explained.

'Honey. Is that dress made of cobwebs or what?'

Sheree turned to look up at him, her smile frozen along with her arms which she still held out at her sides.

'What do you mean?'

Already the suspicion was there. As she dropped her arms to her side, she waited for Max to confirm what she thought the problem was.

'You're giving them a top-rate performance. They can see your tits and they can see your pussy. Where the hell did you get that dress?'

Sheree gasped, then stepped quickly back from the spotlight.

Animated by embarrassment, she stepped back from the limelight, her eyes flitting swiftly from side to side.

'Follow me,' she heard Max say.

He eased her back through the midnight-blue velvet curtains at the back of the stage.

Sheree was breathing hard, not quite knowing whether to revel in her triumphant reception, or remonstrate that they were only interested in her body. And yet, she knew the latter was not true. It couldn't be true. She knew her voice was good.

'You sang real well,' Max commented.

'Thanks for saying so. I really needed for you to say that.'

'It's the truth. Listen to that crowd. They like everything about you, honey. They like the way you sing – and . . .'

He eyed her up and down.

'And they certainly like the way you look. Can't say I

blame them. I like the way you look too.'

He smiled.

She smiled back.

A faraway look came into Max's eyes.

'I was thinking,' he began.

'Of Emmeline?'

He hesitated before nodding. 'Yes. Does it show that much?'

Sheree lightly caressed his cheek. 'You might be cooing sweet words to me, turtle dove, but I can see your thoughts are flying someways up north.'

A sad, regretful look came to his face. 'I'm sorry.'

'No need to be. I understand. I never thought I'd admit it, but I'm sure missing Errol. That's why I know how you feel. Kind of similar aren't we.'

He gazed at her for a moment as if a great realisation had come on him. Then he smiled again, but only fleetingly. He nodded.

'We are that, I suppose. But please, believe me, I wouldn't want to hurt you. Us getting together like we have, I can't say it doesn't exactly mean nothing, but it isn't the same as me and Emmeline – if you know what I mean.'

Sheree patted his big, broad shoulders and felt the mighty muscles tense.

'I know exactly what you mean. I think, for the time being, that we have a need for each other. Once Errol and Emmeline are around, things will probably be different. But for now, let's not get hung up about it. Let's just take some comfort from it whilst we can. OK?'

Max looked straight into her eyes. It made her feel good to see respect reflected in his.

'OK,' he answered. 'Shall I walk you home? It's a fine evening. Still warm out there where the other folks live.'

'Sure. If you'll give me time to change.'

Perhaps it was the night air and the thought of having Max for company, but Sheree did not put her underwear on. Neither did she bother with a dress. Instead, she merely slipped on a silky soft coat; a mixture of silk and linen that was cool against her naked flesh.

Of course, she kept her stockings on, and her shoes which were suede and a pale lilac in colour.

'No Rene?' she asked as Max took her arm.

'Haven't seen him nor Stacey. Might have already left, or might have gone on to some speakeasy with friends. Either way, they ain't trailing us.'

'You make them sound like Indian scouts out tracking for General Custer.'

'Don't you know that I'm really a blonde beneath this?' he laughed as he raised his hat.

Sheree laughed with him and the ease of their companionship with each other made them walk closer.

Max put his arm around her and pulled her closer so that their hips brushed gently against each other.

Max took a deep breath, then moaned and stopped in his tracks.

'Why do you always do this on such a fine night?' he asked, throwing his head back and moaning again.

'What have I done?' Sheree asked, her voice and her expression suddenly anxious.

'Your smell,' he murmured, turning towards her and holding her close. 'You smell gorgeous.'

He kissed her then and she felt the warmth of his palms

through the fabric of her coat.

Already aroused because the night air was drifting up between her legs and caressing her thighs, her desire increased. The touch of his hands was pressing the cool fabric against her bare flesh. And, of course, he didn't know she was naked beneath her coat. But he would soon, she promised herself. He would soon.

'Let's find a place,' she murmured.

'My place or yours?'

She shook her head emphatically. 'No. Not that kind of place.' She glanced up and down the street as if searching for something or someone.

There were still a few people about – just enough to make what was to come that much more interesting.

At the sound of hoof beats, an immediate idea came into Sheree's mind.

'Let's take a cab,' she cried suddenly.

Max was not given enough time to answer.

A horse-drawn, open-top carriage was coming down the street, the sort of transport that seems to belong in the French Quarter of New Orleans far more than a car ever can.

Seeing Sheree waving her hand high, the driver pulled up, the smell of horse sweat and rich leather pungent on the evening air.

'My place,' Sheree cried, and leapt up into the carriage.

'One two one seven, Rue de la Fontaine,' Max instructed the driver.

'The long way round,' Sheree added.

Max stared at her. Somehow, she couldn't bring herself to tell him that talking about Errol had made her feel sad.

Suddenly, she was no longer the exuberant, sexy songbird that Rene Brabonne had hired.

She was a young girl from the sticks of Louisiana, missing the man she loved, but determined to drown her sorrows in the arms of a man who was missing his love too.

She snuggled close to him, nuzzled his chest, and purred with contentment as she enjoyed the warmth of his breath against her hair.

He raised her lips to his, kissed her long and deep and, as he did so, began to undo the buttons of her coat.

He sucked in his breath as his fingers came into contact with her breasts.

He had an urge to say something, but the driver was too near. OK, he was probably used to having lovers cooing on the back seat of his cab, but it looked as if Sheree intended to do a lot more than coo.

Not that the driver seemed to care that his passengers were breathing heavy and groaning slightly. His gaze stared straight ahead, somewhere between the horses ears, and his own ears seemed only to hear the clip clop of the horse's hoofs, their echo ricocheting off the closed shutters and dark buildings that lined their route home.

Invitingly, Sheree lay herself back on the seat of the cab. Her eyes told Max everything he needed to know.

Her coat was spread out around her. Her body was bare and his for the taking.

People walked by on the sidewalks. Sheree wondered if they surmised what Max was doing. Could they know he was kissing her breasts, sucking her nipples into his mouth, licking and nibbling on them before his lips went to her belly.

Could they possibly know that his fingers were running through her pubic hair.

She moaned as he squeezed her pubic lips. There was a glorious sensuality in feeling the warm, heavy air lying on her naked flesh. She was exposed to the night and to any eyes that might be watching from the dark windows along their route.

But she didn't care. She almost wanted them to see, invited them to gaze upon her firm, young form.

Perhaps the young would be jealous of what was happening to her. Perhaps the old would be disgusted. Or perhaps, just perhaps, the old would be roused to old memories. The husband might return to bed to gaze on a wife who now cursed him instead of kissing him. And the widow might return to a lonely bed to reflect on how things used to be, on how she had loved, was loved, and made love.

As they travelled home, Max played with her body, caressing her, squeezing her, cupping her breasts and exploring her sex.

He slid his fingers into her, the wetness covering his fingers, running down over his fist.

Sheree raised her buttocks off the seat as delicious sensations spread like racing quicksilver.

Her sex was like a cauldron rich in spices, herbs and honey. Steam in the form of desire, was spilling out from her deepest depths, rising, spreading throughout her trembling body.

She closed her eyes, revelling in the wickedness of it all, hoping that someone high in some window was looking out on the street below. What would they think, she wondered? Here she was spread semi-naked in the open-topped carriage. And there was Max, exploring her body with his hands and his lips.

She also wanted someone in the street to know what she was doing, but it would not have been so easy for them to see, though of course, they would hear her.

At exactly that time when her body could no longer contain the nervous energy aroused by Max's fingers, Sheree cried out the sound of climax.

She could not see who responded. Could not see what surprised looks fell her way. She only smiled to herself, purring as the last ebb and flow of orgasm drifted like a falling tide.

In her mind, she was still the performer and was still performing.

Even as Max mounted her, spilt his semen into her, and growled his climax along with the last heave of his loins, she kept her eyes shut.

Errol had been on her mind earlier, but performing in a dress that was obviously transparent, and seeing what was in other people's minds, her thoughts went back to Rene and Stacey.

Along with Stacey, she had watched herself doing things with Rene.

Had she really done things with Rene? She couldn't remember doing much so far and, if she had, she certainly couldn't remember Stacey being there.

I wonder, she thought, *am I aware that Stacey wants to watch me having sex with her husband, or is it me? Is it me who* wants *Stacey to watch me having sex with her husband?*

Chapter 13

It was when Stacey McKendrick had realised that good looks were all she had, and her voice would never be her fortune, that she'd aimed at becoming Mrs Brabonne.

Of course, the idea of having a wife had never entered Rene's head. Why should it? He had the looks and the status to ensure that he would always be successful with women.

When Stacey had first come to him saying she wanted to be a singer, he hadn't even asked to hear her voice. He had just looked her up and down, assessing how one so young seemed so worldly wise.

So Rene had seduced her before she'd sang in front of the clientele of the Catnip Club. Or so he thought. If he had considered the matter a little more thoroughly and wasn't so egoistic, he would have realised that Stacey had seduced him.

However, it soon became apparent that Stacey could not sing and neither could she dance. Therefore, he should have told her to go immediately, but he didn't. Something about her proved irresistible to him, and so she became his right-hand woman. She looked after his employees, both male and female – and in more ways than one. And she catered for his ego – and his other more hedonistic tastes. Stacey, it had to be said, became his procurer. His pimp.

Not that it was always a case of getting girls for him to take to his bed. Rene's sexual tastes, Stacey perceived, were far more wide ranging than that. He had a curiosity about the more perverse side of sexuality and, by catering for this, Stacey got beneath his skin. She became something and someone he could not do without so, just in case she ran off with one of the young studs she so ably seduced, he married her. 'And now,' he had boasted, 'you have become one of my chattels.'

Stacey had smiled at that, but said nothing.

Sheree was one of those delights Rene enjoyed with able assistance from Stacey. He congratulated himself on taking her on. Unlike Stacey, she really could sing. Besides that, she was very attractive, in fact, she was definitely the most exotic creature he had ever seen.

Sheree was not the first young woman to live in the apartment above that of the Brabonnes. It had always been his pleasure to watch unobserved as his protégés had undressed before his eyes, or made love with one of their men friends.

He had presumed Sheree would do very much the same thing. He had not expected her to use the tobacco store statue as a pseudo lover, but the fact that she got her sexual release for something that wasn't real was oddly arousing. The plain fact was, he was becoming besotted with her and what she did. Luckily for him, Stacey, as always, helped him enjoy it more.

As he viewed the slender young woman through the clever mirror lately patented by some guy over in Houston,

Stacey was knelt between his legs, her mouth and her hands encouraging his erection to blossom.

Above her, Rene breathed heavily. His eyes felt heavy. He wanted to close them because of what Stacey was doing to him. Her tongue was licking around the head of his penis. Her fingers were fondling his balls and pulling on his length, teasing both blood and semen to rush to its tip.

But he could not close his eyes. He wanted to watch Sheree carry out her nightly regular routine with the tobacco store statue.

He took a deep breath, his chest expanding as if to make room for his pounding heart. There was a thudding in his head. Sweat glistened on his forehead and ran gently into his eyebrows. Even when a droplet of sweat trickled down his cheek, he did not avert his gaze from the scene before him. Sheree was making love to her statue again.

Each undulation she made on her wooden lover was accompanied by soft, mewing cries of wonder, delight, and sheer abandon. As her hips gyrated, she threw her head back and fondled her own breasts. So piquant, so delectable was the scene of this slim young woman, back arched and eyes closed, that Rene almost forgot that it was Stacey's mouth around his penis. In his mind it was Sheree's vagina.

'That's it, baby,' he was saying. 'That's it. Take it in. Relax. Let it come.'

He groaned when he came, his eyes narrowed as he watched the object of his desire do the same in the other room. It was as if, he thought, there were only the two of them in the whole building; that there was no wall between them, and that Stacey wasn't there either.

Even when Sheree was no longer in the room through the

mirror, Rene continued to stare.

Stacey had given good account of herself as usual and he had climaxed easily, encouraged by her considerable expertise. And yet, he felt oddly unfulfilled. He had a tremendous urge to be more intimate with his latest chanteuse. Not just to feel her naked body beneath him. He wanted more than that. He wanted to know that she was near, to smell her perfume, her femininity, and hear silk rustle suggestively and know that she was behind him.

Placing her hands on his knees, Stacey pulled herself up to face him. She kissed him on the mouth and he smelt his own gender. He didn't like it.

'Please don't.' He turned his head. Her kiss landed on his cheek.

Stacey's face darkened. 'Don't do this to me, Rene!'

He blinked before looking at her. 'What do you mean?'

'Don't come the innocent, Rene. I know you. I'm married to you. I've observed every little emotion that's ever crossed your face or been in your eyes. I know when you're falling in love. You did once with me. Remember?'

Rene took her face between his hands.

'And I still love you, my darling.'

A deep frown furrowed Stacey's brow. There was anger in her eyes, venom on her tongue.

'You'd better still love me, Rene Brabonne. You'd better still love me or it'll be the worse for you, so help me!'

The smile that had been playing round Rene's mouth turned to a sneer. His fingers tightened on her jaw and her cheeks and a dark hardness came to his eyes.

Stacey pulled at his hands.

'Rene! You're hurting me! Stop it!'

Rene's face came close to hers.

'Understand me, dear wife. No male member of my family is used to being given orders by some female member. You knew my habits and my passions before you married me. You thought you were my mistress as well as my wife. You cannot be that. A mistress is always obeyed and, for a time, I did obey you. But not any more. I am out of my kennel and I will run any hare to ground that I choose!'

Stacey had never seen such anger in her husband's eyes before. Even her usual bravado seemed unwilling to rise to the surface and do battle with him.

Fear rose in Stacey's heart and became etched on her face. Rene was indeed slipping his leash. Stacey was in danger of losing her husband.

When he at last loosened his grip, she jerked her head away.

'You're going to take her out there, aren't you?'

She used both hands to rub at her reddened cheeks and her frown didn't go away.

Adjusting his clothes as he did so, Rene rose to his feet.

Stacey stayed kneeling as she looked up at him.

Rene was smiling, but not with happiness. There was a hint of contempt around his mouth and something unpleasant in his eyes.

A weak woman would have shivered, but Stacey was not a weak woman.

Rene laughed.

'That's right. I'm going to take her back to my roots. I'm going to give her a taste of all that has gone before in my family. Sometime in the past, the history of my family might well have been bound up with hers – judging by her appearance. Don't you think so, my darling Stacey?'

Stacey glowered.

'You don't?'

Rene began to laugh again. 'Well, I am afraid it will not make too much difference, *ma chérie*. What I want, I get. What I will do, I will do.'

'You'll regret it, Rene,' Stacey growled in a low, threatening voice. 'I swear to you, you'll live to regret it.'

But Rene had already left her. He had strode out of the door and he was whistling. She'd heard that tune before. Knew what was on his mind. Knew what his intentions were. She also knew she had no chance of stopping him.

Chapter 14

The train broke down in some godforsaken place that Emmeline had never heard of. She supposed she was in Kentucky or Tennessee judging by the scenery, but she hadn't really been taking a great deal of notice of town, county or state signs after her experience in the luggage car.

All she knew was that this place was pretty dusty, but well nourished by water judging by the amount of birch and maple growing around.

'Have I got time to stretch my legs?' she asked the conductor.

He looked her up and down. Apparently liking what he saw, he gave her a white-toothed smile.

'Stretch anything you want, ma'am. If you've a mind.'

He raised his eyebrows suggestively.

She raised hers as though he had just uttered naughty little words that no decent lady should ever hear. But he probably knew she was no decent lady. Hell, who wanted to be that anyways?

The heat hit her as she alighted from the train and she pulled her sunhat down close to her face so she didn't have to squint to see her whereabouts. She'd also heard or read somewhere that wrinkles come easy in strong sunlight.

There was a clapperboard station building beside the track. Nothing remotely resembling the white painted type of buildings you might see in Maine or Virginia – it was far too dilapidated for that. The window panes were cracked and the rain guttering and drainpipe leaned too far away from the roof to ever be of any use.

Here and there the termites and the weather had eaten through the layered wood. Someone had tried patching it up with odd bits taken from some other construction judging by the variety of differing colours and textures. In a way the odd bits matched because, like the building, they were flaking and dry as cinder.

Chickens in search of scattered crumbs poked their heads through handy holes. There was something macabre about their bodies being left out in the open, a ghostly enactment of their eventual fate.

Emmeline turned away from them and strolled a little. A dust-laden breeze clutched at her skirt and made it rustle and swish up over her knees. It was pale blue with pink and red roses scattered over it. She wore a matching blue scarf around her hat which was also caught by the breeze and blown across her face.

The sound of clucking chickens mixed with that of a rickety rocker as it squeaked back and forth on the porch, the boards beneath it squealing in reply.

Emmeline eyed its occupant, but he didn't eye her. He seemed more interested in the iron beast that sat belching steam as the engineers shouted, clanged heavy tools against unyielding metal, and swore in violet streams at the locomotive's intractability.

'I think I'll just take a walk down by them trees,' she muttered once she'd made her mind up the loco was taking no notice of either the men's language or their mechanical know how.

Before taking a step, she pressed her hat down more firmly on her head and made a swift decision about direction.

There was a path leading through a gap in the trees. It wasn't a proper path, just a track made by animals and people that had eroded the grass and left the red clay hard and bare.

Once under the canopy of high trees, she felt almost sleepy. Only the thought of the guard and his love hate relationship with leather kept her from lying down in the grass and dozing off completely. She hadn't gone back to visit him, although he had asked her if she would. Once, she had decided, was enough. Besides, she wanted some time to think about her and Max. There was a burning in her that only Max could ignite into a flame. As sexually liberated as she was, there was something between her and that big black trumpet player that she couldn't get away from. What was more, she was going back to it. It was only Rene that had put a distance between her and Max. Rene with his soft words about her doing better in the Big Apple than she could ever do in New Orleans. He might well be right. But it didn't really matter any more. She didn't care if some English lord was drooling over her. It was Max she wanted.

As she walked, she trailed her fingers over the foliage that fringed the path and kissed her face and her hair.

At last, the lure of the cool green grass and chunks of dark ferns were too much to resist.

Train journeys made her hot and weren't designed to be comfortable or interesting, that much was for sure. They were purely a method of getting from A to B until something better turned up. Cars were OK, but not always reliable. Perhaps, she mused, aeroplanes would be the thing of the future that would take her from one end of the continent to the other. But not if she had to get up in them leather hats and goggles that all the famous flyers sported when they posed for photographs and such.

Perhaps it might be aeroplanes, she said to herself as she peeled her dress from off her shoulders and let it fall quivering to her feet.

She was about to lie down wearing only her underwear, but stopped suddenly.

She looked around her, narrowing her eyes so she could see more clearly into the darker shadows that squatted beneath the trees.

I'm alone, she thought to herself. *All alone*. It felt kind of nice.

Smiling, she stretched her arms above her head so that her camisole rode up above her waist. Then, as though she were dancing like she had done at the Cotton Club and the Catnip Club before it, she peeled her silk top over her head and, once it was free, flung it to one side.

Her bare breasts tingled. She looked down at them and, pleased with their shape and the brazen way her nipples were reacting to the air, she wriggled her torso so that they jiggled and swayed from side to side.

She laughed, then studied them more seriously because they seemed to be begging her to. Tantalising tingles reminiscent of icy, unseen fingers caressed each enticing orb. An odd ache played around her nipples, inviting her fingers to touch them, to feel the hardness of their core and the softness of their surrounding halos.

She flicked at them with her fingers, then her thumbs. Her lips parted. Her breath quickened.

Closing her eyes, she stretched her arms above her head again, then, moving like the dancer she was, she lowered them and slowly undid the buttons of the pale blue satin items that hid her lower torso.

As she did so, she hummed a favourite tune and pretended that the bushes and trees were her audience all there for a private viewing. *Today*, cried the master of ceremonies, who of course only lived in her head, *you will see far more of Emmeline Emerald than you have ever seen before*.

Softly, with hardly a whisper of sound, her lace-trimmed cami-knickers fell to her ankles. Emmeline kicked them to one side, wiggled her hips, then threw her arms into the air.

'Dah-dah!' She sang the words as if she were taking a final encore. A flock of birds scattered from the nearest tree.

Dropping her arms to her sides, she slowly lowered herself onto the silky grass and murmured as its silky softness caressed her flesh.

Head resting on arms, she stretched and closed her eyes so she could more fully appreciate the coolness and texture of her bed.

By closing her eyes, she blotted out her surroundings, and yet they were more real to her somehow. It was as if Nature itself were touching her, caressing her breasts and blowing at her pubic hair with a gentle, warm breath.

Because her most recent sexual encounter had been with the guard in the luggage van, she had trouble evicting him from her mind. It wasn't the guard she wanted to be there. It was Max who loved her. Max who was easily controlled, yet played her body with as much skill as he played his trumpet.

The grass kissed her flesh. The breeze played over her body more softly than human hand could ever do. Suddenly, something a little more intense than the breeze touched her nipple. It was still fragile. Still incredibly light, yet more tangible than the shifting of the air.

Blue wings fluttered before her open eyes. The most beautiful of butterflies was perched on her nipple, its wings gently fanning the dulcet air.

Hardly daring to breathe, but unable to stop her breast from gently rising and falling, Emmeline watched as the creature moved its feathery legs, preened its lengthy antennae.

Another one joined the first, its touch making her tense her muscles reflexively as it moved hesitantly up and down her stomach. The first butterfly turned in the direction of the second as if it had heard it land.

Could butterflies hear? She wasn't sure. But she could see that they were moving towards each other, the first gently flapping its wings as its spidery legs moved down her breasts.

The wings of the second butterfly didn't move quite so much as it moved closer to the first.

As Emmeline watched, it came to her that the two insects resembled her and Max. One had been set on a pinnacle above the other. They had separated, encouraged by a third source.

A dark cloud seemed to pass between Emmeline and the

shafts of sunlight that pierced through the overhead trees as Rene and his ancestral home came suddenly to her mind.

His home was grand as were all the homes of Southern gentlemen, even those whose ancestry was not honest to good English speaking.

But although his home was painted white, there was a darkness to its heart; a scarlet decadence that was at first oddly alluring and then slightly repugnant.

But you escaped it, she told herself with some pride. *Your duke or earl, or whatever he was, did a deal on your behalf. Your new boss went along with it, and now you're as free as a bird.*

Unwilling to disturb her fluttering guests for a few minutes, Emmeline closed her eyes and tried to regain the pleasant feelings she had experienced when first lying down here.

But the spell had been broken. It was almost impossible not to see the things she didn't want to see. There were bars all around her. She was like a captured canary within a cage, her life dictated by someone who considered it his privilege to do so, and her duty to obey.

The bars disappeared. Now a mass of hands surrounded her. Men touched her intimately, treating her as though they were bidding a price like she was some piece of meat or some thoroughbred mare.

She writhed and struggled to get away from their clawing fingers. But she felt them on her breasts, squeezing them, cupping them. She felt them on her belly, pushing her legs apart, feeling what was between, pushing their fingers into her, trailing them down between her buttocks, testing their firmness.

'No,' she was crying. 'No!'

And suddenly, the dream was left behind. She was crying out for real.

She sat up quickly, so quickly that the two butterflies took flight and flew away.

'No,' she whimpered, her eyes sad as she watched them go and felt the wetness of tears upon her cheeks. 'No.'

Her breasts quivered as she shook with sobs. Max had watched that crowd doing that to her and had been unable to do anything about it. He had also been unable to buy her contract back from Rene.

'One year,' Rene had said. 'Only one year.' But Rene had lied.

She had stayed in New York for one year and had done all that was required of her. She had been outraged when she was told that Rene had signed her contract for two years. She would still be serving out that contract now if it hadn't been for her English duke. He had bought it out. She was free. New York was now behind her.

She'd been so excited once her time was up at last and had written to Max straightaway. At first she had asked him to meet her halfway and had been surprised when he'd refused.

'I want you to come here,' he'd written.' I want you to face up to what happened. To your fear. To everything.'

She had not understood at first. Only now were things beginning to come clear, and clearest of all were the facial features of her darling Max.

'I'm coming for you, Max,' she cried out to the trees. 'I'm coming for you!'

Chapter 15

Amber was rubbing at Errol's wrists with a special cold cream that she said she'd made up herself. The manacles that had lately held his wrists were now lying on the floor beside him.

'That's good,' Amber murmured as, with his free hand, he massaged her breast.

'I'm glad you like it,' he said before kissing her.

Her mouth opened beneath his, the lips hot and juicy, her tongue dextrous in its determination to enter his mouth.

Errol did not protest that he didn't like such probing tongues. His heart was pounding in his chest. He knew instinctively that the time was close when he could escape this place. Amber trusted him. Not only that, but he had discovered a chink in her dominating armour. Soon, if he moved quickly but carefully, he would be free.

'Do you like this too?' he asked as he took her nipple between his thumb and forefinger.

Her response was exactly as he'd expected. She groaned and, with the hardening and lengthening of her nipple, he sensed a perceptible weakening in her willpower.

'Oh, stop!' she moaned. 'Stop.'

Her response was so powerful that her whole body writhed, and her back arched, pushing her magnificent breast more firmly into his hand.

'You make me weak, you naughty boy. You shouldn't be doing this!' But her voice wavered. Amber, he had noticed early on, was one of those women who became completely and utterly abandoned once their nipples were being played with.

In the past Errol had read about the Greek hero Achilles whose weakest spot had been his heel. In Amber's case, her nipples were to blame. Once they were touched and being fondly manipulated, she was putty in anyone's hands.

Amber groaned without shame, and Errol wondered if the voluptuous redhead had any real need for genital contact to bring about an orgasm. It was as if her nipples were triggers to the whole of her sexual being and Errol could not help but be intrigued and even aroused by her reactions.

'Wicked boy!' Amber exclaimed, but made no attempt to push him away.

She lay back upon her cushions, her silk robe open, her eyes closed.

Errol took it as both an invitation and an opportunity.

He rested his chin on her belly as he used both hands to manipulate her nipples.

Being a man of vibrant passions, Errol could not help the fact that his penis was fit to burst against the stiff leather of the cock harness.

Bear with it, he told himself. *Keep it under control.*

'Put it in me!' Amber suddenly cried out.

Errol did not alter position. His mind was working fast.

His fingers were pulling on the pebble-hard nipples that were burning hot beneath his touch.

'Put it in me, you sonofabitch!' Amber shouted.

His judgement had been correct. Amber really was coming without him being in her. Yet she still wanted the illusion of having been shafted by him.

He judged she was now at her weakest; her most vulnerable.

Now! He thought to himself. *Now!*

His hands left her breasts. He slid down to the floor, then made as if to get up, to push his pelvis against hers and send his shaft into her welcoming niche.

Instead, he grabbed the fallen manacles.

Amber struggled and cried out as he fastened the metal bands around her wrists.

'Stop!' she cried out. 'I will not allow this! I will punish you! I will beat you till you bleed!'

There was a metal post behind her lounger, a support for the glass roof above their heads. He passed the chain behind that so she couldn't strike out at him.

Only her legs and her voice now fought against him.

'You bastard!' she cried, her legs flailing as he fought to bring her wild kicks under control. 'Let me go. Let me go or I'll . . .'

More exultant than any warrior, Errol brought his face close to hers. There was a golden gleam in his eyes now and a wild happiness all over his face.

'Now hush that foul mouth, Amber honey,' he said in the sort of way he'd heard share croppers use.

'Don't you dare speak to me like that!'

'You don't want to be quiet?' Errol raised his eyebrows in

mock surprise. 'Well in that case honey-child, I'll have to shut it for you.'

Amber's eyes opened wide as Errol fastened the same gag he had worn since his captivity around his former mistress's mouth.

All the while, Amber struggled and kicked, her body lifting from the lounger, her breasts flopping wildly around, and her hips gyrating beneath him.

He took the key from a side table and unfastened the manacles from around his ankles and transferred them to hers. It restricted the movement of her legs to some extent, but not enough to fully placate the shame he had felt since she had first imprisoned him.

He looked around the room for something to inspire him. As his eyes alighted on a blue and white porcelain dish piled high with fruit, a smile enveloped his face.

'This,' he said taking hold of a banana, 'is exactly what I need.' Still smiling lasciviously, he turned to her. 'And it's exactly what you need too, honey.'

Amber began to struggle.

'Now come on, Amber honey. I know you better than that. I know you want it.'

Amber's eyes regarded him now with pure hate as she struggled to avoid what was about to happen to her. But Errol felt no sympathy. She would take what he was giving her and take it gladly.

There was a hint of wickedness in his eyes as he approached her.

He held the thick, yellow fruit before her eyes so she was in no doubt of what was about to happen to her. But still she struggled.

'Now come on, honey,' said Errol, leaning on one elbow as he spoke. 'I know what buttons to push. You'll beg me to put this piece of stiffness in you. You know that.'

Amber merely struggled again.

Errol smiled. He continued to hold the banana in front of her eyes with one hand. With the other he began to play with her right nipple.

The effect was electric. At his touch, Amber began arching her back. As ecstasy began to take hold of her, she bent her knees in an effort to open her legs because her ankles were restrained by the manacles.

'Easy does it, baby,' Errol murmured.

As he continued to finger her nipples, he slid the tip of the banana between her pubic lips.

Despite her confinement, Amber began throwing her head from side to side, and her body, unable to resist, trembled with pleasure.

Not once did Amber attempt to close her legs as he pushed the hard, under-ripe fruit into her. To Errol's delighted amazement, she actually lifted her bottom and bent her knees that bit more.

Soon, the whole of the fruit had disappeared. Amber, Errol decided, was enjoying this far too much, and that hadn't exactly been the point of the exercise.

He glanced down at his own penis.

'Traitor,' he muttered.

Restricted by the size of his erect penis, his balls had a mauvish sheen. His glans was moist, and his whole length was throbbing with anticipation.

'Get down boy!' he ordered. 'You're not going where you think you're going.'

A sudden thought came to him as he studied the way his genitals were behaving. He also remembered the plug attached to the strap that ran between his buttocks.

A hint of sudden meanness came to his face. His hand fell away from Amber's breast and he left the banana to do its own fucking.

Quickly, with fingers that seemed too big to do anything, he undid the buckle that held the cock harness in place. Once it was off, dangling in his hand, he looked directly into the eyes of the woman who had forced him to wear it.

'Do you see this, honey?' He shook it so the leather danced and the buckles jangled. 'This is an item of shame as well as pleasure. And now it's your turn. You were the mistress, I was the slave. Now I'm the master, and you're the slave. Savvy?'

Wide-eyed, Amber stared at the harness. She began to struggle.

Errol snuggled up close. He had her measure. He knew what soothed her.

Smiling triumphantly, he again resorted to tweaking the most sensitive part of her body.

He played with each nipple in turn, pressing it, twisting it, pulling it and pinching it.

Once she was compliant and almost sobbing with desire, his fingers left her flesh to deal quickly and decisively with the leather harness that she was now to wear.

He took great pleasure in pushing the anal plug into her body and tightening the strap that held it to the waistband. The piece at the front had been made for male genitalia so did not sit well against her pubic lips.

'Damn it,' he swore. 'This has to fit right, otherwise that

piece of fruit you got in there is going to slide right out.'

Again his eyes went to the fruit dish for enlightenment. The solution was easy. He got hold of two shiny, red apples, put both into the pouch made for a set of cock and balls, and fastened the strap into the front of the waistband.

Once it was all in place and the apples were held tight against her sex, he went back to playing with Amber's nipples.

'Don't that feel so good?' he murmured between planting kisses in her cleavage.

Because his fingers were again twiddling with her teats, Amber began to surrender once more to her sensations.

'Make the most of it, honey,' he said, continuing to play with her nipples as he took his penis in his other hand. 'This is the last you'll see of me.'

To Errol, it was the strangest sex he'd ever had in his life.

Amber, assisted by the assortment of fruit and Errol's fingers, achieved her orgasm at exactly the same time as Errol spurted his semen over her belly.

He didn't bother to untie her or clean his emission from off her snow-white flesh. He merely washed and dressed himself as quickly as he could and took what dollars he thought the woman owed him for services rendered.

Pierre attempted to stop him from going, then stepped back once he saw the furious determination in his eyes.

'I've given her what she wanted, and this time she got more than she bargained for,' he said before leaving.

Pierre stood dumbstruck for a moment before he saw the handful of dollars Errol held in his hand.

'I'll call the police,' he blurted.

Errol grabbed him by the shirt collar.

'One word, and I'll call them right now. Imagine the gossip in this town if your mistress was seen trussed up like a thanksgiving turkey, stuffed with fruit and garnished with sauce.'

Pierre's eyes flickered nervously. He licked his lips.

Errol could see that Pierre had exercised some judgement.

Whistling happily, he went out of the door and strolled off down the garden path, his jacket slung over his shoulder in exactly the same manner as when he'd arrived. With some luck he'd find a bus going out of this place right away. He had no wish to linger. New Orleans was his next stop, and hopefully it was there that he'd find Shirley Anne.

Chapter 16

It was a wild night at the Catnip Club. Max was belting out one helluva jazz number that set people dancing as though they'd just drunk the bar dry.

Women wearing gauzy hats, similar in shape to tight-fitting flower pots, swung their arms and legs and pretended that they were sweet young things rather than women who had reached their zenith just before the Great War. Skirts swirled and strings of beads that reached their hips swung out in the opposite direction to their arms. They were for all the world like animated clocks, the strings of beads swinging like pendulums.

A lot of loud cheering and clapping greeted the end of his tune and sweaty bodies regained chairs and ordered more bourbon, more champagne, and more food.

The lights above the small stage on which the band sat became more subdued and changed from red to dark blue.

Sheree, wearing only the mauve silk dress, walked slowly out onto the stage, her head down, her movements sultry and incredibly erotic.

Soulful and enigmatic, the notes from Max's trumpet began to play in time with her movements.

At first she stood sideways on to the audience, the geometric line of her haircut falling forward over her face as she waited for her cue.

This was a new song she was singing tonight; the sultriest, sexiest song she had ever sung in her life, and she was dressed – or rather – undressed to suit it.

Just as Rene had ordered, she wore no underwear beneath the plainly cut dress. Only the rustle of silk against silk betrayed the fact that she was wearing stockings.

At the right time, with the right note, she turned her face towards the audience. Her eyes were sharply defined with black, mauve and dark pink make-up. Peek-a-boo fashion through her hair, they peered at the audience, offering plenty, and firing them with a need to know more.

The small sounds that pervade a nightclub disappeared once the words of her song rang out and caught hold of their minds.

> 'You send shivers down my spine,
> My body aches for you all the time.
> Run your hands through my hair,
> You can have me anywhere, but baby,
> Be kind to me.'

A brittle hush descended. Only the sensual sound of Max's trumpet and her voice echoed around the darkened room. Even the barmen stopped serving to lean on the bar and listen, then ogle her as she turned full frontal to belt out the last two verses.

A gasp of astonishment rippled through the audience. It was like an orgasm; a joint anticipation of climax that flowed like the sea kissing a shingle beach.

Sheree did not acknowledge the reason for the sudden gasp. Resolved to concentrate on the delivery of the song, she stared straight ahead like some ancient painted idol. But she did know what they were gasping about.

Affected by the dark blue light, the lighter blue of her dress became almost transparent. Even without looking down at herself, she could see what the audience was seeing.

Her nipples were like ripe grapes, prominent behind the thin silk that covered them. The silk sheath accentuated the shape of her hips, her thighs, and her waistline and the triangle of darkness between the tops of her legs.

Her dress, her hair and her whole body seemed to shimmer as she reached the climax of her song.

As she sang, Sheree let her gaze travel lazily over those gathered until finally alighting on Rene.

He was standing at the back in semi-darkness. Beside him was a bigger man who had small eyes that were half hidden in above fleshy cheeks.

Her gaze merely skimmed the heavier man. It was Rene's mind she wanted to look into. She wanted to see if her person was as clear in his mind as it had been. Was she still submitting to his most perverse demands?

To her surprise, his thoughts seemed slightly confused, the visions hazy. It was as though he no longer knew himself what he wanted her for. She could also tell that he didn't want anyone else to know he was disturbed by her. Something in his make-up had been changed by her presence. So far, she did not know what but felt in time that she would.

Once the last note had hit the ceiling, she turned herself sideways to the audience again in one swift movement, her hair concealing her face, one knee bent, one hand resting on it in a classic Art-Nouveau pose.

The audience leapt to its feet, clapping, cheering and crying for more.

Rene too was looking very happy, but with far more reserve than his clientele.

The man with him was tapping at a scarred cheek with a silver-topped cane, his gaze fixed on the woman Rene called Sheree, but whose real name was Shirley Anne.

'Is she not as good as I said she was?'

The man nodded and smiled sardonically in answer to Rene's question.

'What will you be asking?'

Rene smiled and took a silver pocket watch from his vest. 'Now that is a leading question, Richthof. You know her contract will be auctioned to the highest bidder along with her body.'

The man he'd addressed as Richthof glanced at him sidelong. 'I don't respond well to people who refuse me what I want.'

Rene kept his eyes on the stage. Sheree had gone and Max was belting out some real hot mamma of a Black Bottom arrangement.

'Neither do the other interested parties who will be attending my auction. Please bear in mind that you are the one who have had a foretaste of what is in store for the lucky purchaser. Only you have had the privilege of watching her from my private room.'

'And liking what I see ... Yes, yes. I take your point. I

also take it that this auction will be in the usual place?'

Trying his best not to smile too triumphantly, Rene nodded. 'The Brabonne Plantation. As always.'

'As always,' repeated the man, his eyes searching the stage and the room for the lovely creature he had seen and heard earlier. There was a sharp tap as the tip of his cane hit the floor. He turned to Rene, a purposeful look on his face.

'I'm determined I shall have her, Brabonne. Mark my words. I am very determined.'

'I always said you were a man of taste, Richthof. My little Sheree sings like a bird does she not?'

Richthof laughed. 'It's not her singing I want her for. I want her to perform with me like she does with that statue she's got in her room. God, but I'll get her rolling I will. I'll give her body some performing once she's mine.'

Rene hid his contempt for the big Austrian immigrant behind the smoke-screen of his latest cigar.

He did not entirely approve of the man, and he certainly didn't like him. Besides that, he couldn't help feeling he'd prefer Sheree to go to someone less of an animal than Richthof.

He shrugged. What was it to him? She was another little strumpet with a big ego and an average voice. Average? He corrected himself. No. Not average. Sheree had a beautiful voice. A beautiful body too, and he couldn't help but notice that.

The trouble was, Stacey had noticed as well, and Rene had grown accustomed to the routine of his life. His wife was useful to him and knew well.

'You'll get as fed up of this one as you have of all the others,' she said.

She's probably right, he thought to himself. All the same, he couldn't help but regret the fact that Sheree had to go.

Sheree was taking off her make-up and wore only a pale pink wrap when Rene came in to see her.

He smiled at her reflection in the mirror and placed his hands on her shoulders.

'I have something for you,' he said in the kind of tone a father might use to a daughter.

Sheree, who still couldn't quite forget the fact that her real name was Shirley Anne, gazed back at him round-eyed.

'You do?'

She knew she sounded innocent. She always did in Rene's presence. His closeness and the feelings she felt for him made her feel like that. Perhaps it was because having such feelings for him meant she was forgetting Errol. And yet she didn't want to forget Errol. She still loved him. How could she not love a man she had known all her life?

'My darling girl, you are a credit to the Catnip Club. You have the sort of voice that burrows deep into the soul.'

'That's very kind of you to say so.'

Her voice faltered. Rene nodded, his eyes sparkling as though he knew her thoughts as well as she knew his.

He rested his chin on the top of her head and smiled. 'I have a contract for you to sign. One year. That is all I ask of you.'

Sheree's eyes opened wide. 'A singing contract?'

He didn't answer, only went on smiling.

'When do I sign it?'

He straightened up, but his warm palms remained on her shoulders.

'How about tonight over supper. We can celebrate with champagne.'

Sheree agreed and was too excited to ask where they would celebrate. She only knew that Stacey was away and she would have Rene to herself. It was wicked to think so. After all, this was a married man she had in mind. But she couldn't help it.

Have I got more wicked since coming to New Orleans? she asked herself.

Rene had not stipulated where they were to dine, but told her he would be back for her later.

'Get some rest,' he said.

His advice was gladly received. Tonight had been quite a performance, much better than the ordeal she had originally thought it would be.

There was a low pink chaise in her dressing room, so she curled up on that still wearing her pink wrap.

By the time Rene came back, she had slept well and woken refreshed.

'I'm sorry,' she blurted, annoyed with herself for not being ready for him. 'It won't take me a moment to get dressed.'

His hand landed on her shoulder. 'Please. Stay as you are.'

Sheree found it impossible to conceal her surprise.

'But I can't possibly go out like this!'

A vision of her half-naked body entering a high-class restaurant went through her mind.

Rene shook his head. 'We are not going out to some place where pink water is served and bootleg whisky is poured from a white china tea pot. We are celebrating here.

Everyone else has gone, and it will be only you and me. I have even laid on some special entertainment for you.'

Holding her elbow, he guided her out of the door. She let herself be handled by him and there was something oddly comforting in doing so.

The club was strangely quiet and far darker than when it was full.

Their footsteps echoed as he guided her across the alternate dark and light diagonals of the inlaid maple flooring.

We're finding our way almost by instinct, Sheree thought. *It's as though I know each turn between each table, and yet I never leave the stage.*

As though reading her thoughts, Rene tightened his grip on her elbow.

Although all the other chairs were turned upside down on top of their tables, a lone arrangement had been made on a small dias next to a plush red curtain.

Rene pulled the chair back for her before sitting down.

Sheree hugged the silken robe around herself. She felt very vulnerable with this man but, because nothing but silk stood between her and him, she also felt highly aroused.

'To us,' he said as he poured the champagne then raised his glass. 'And especially to you.'

Bubbles of champagne seemed to burst in Sheree's mouth and an airy lightness came to her mind.

She had never touched champagne before coming here. She had never done a lot of other things either.

'Now,' he said, his hand covering hers. 'Let us get down to business.'

Sheree wanted to say, never mind the business, please

Anything Goes

keep touching my hand. But Rene was the boss. He was calling the shots and paying her a salary for standing up on stage, singing sexy songs and looking sexy herself.

He brought out a single page of paper and slid it across the table to her. He took a pen from an inside coat pocket and passed that to her too.

Just as she was about to pick up the pen, he took hold of her hand.

'Drink the glass of champagne first – to seal our contract.'

'I certainly will,' she replied, and together they drank the first two glasses.

The lightness in her head was turning to a thick mist, and the writing on the paper she was signing had suddenly turned into some ancient language she did not understand.

But she signed anyway. It didn't matter what was written there. It could only be in her favour. Nothing could be any worse than living in the back of beyond and being a nobody. Now, she was a star and, although memories of Errol still tugged at her heart strings, tonight the alcohol helped drown him out.

Through a champagne-induced haze, she handed the signed paper back to Rene and, as the second glass reached her lips, she studied him more fully.

I want him, she murmured inwardly, and yet she could not say it out loud. *You've been good to me*, she wanted to say, yet she couldn't.

Suddenly, it was hard to find her voice, that same voice that had earlier sung such a steamy, provocative song. What could she say to him?

'I believe you said something about entertainment.'

She was only vaguely aware of his smile. She cursed herself for not having had the sense to time her drinks more sensibly. But there it was. She was ecstatic; happy to be where she was and to be with who she was with.

Rene snapped his fingers.

Suddenly, two dancers spun onto the floor.

There was no music to accompany them, but then, there didn't need to be.

These were not modern day dancers, but dark-haired, sloe-eyed people who hailed from the Andes, that thick spine of mountains that runs from Mexico down to the tip of Patagonia.

They wore odd tribal outfits that might have been Mayan, or might just as well have been Aztec or Inca.

Aprons of black cloth trimmed with gold hung from their loins. Thick bands of gold encircled their necks and were matched by heavy rings that hung from their ears and their nostrils.

A single, tall red feather stood high from their heads, and gold bells and feathers jangled from their ankles.

Their bodies were muscular, the contours enhanced by the generous provision of oil.

Something about their beauty and her own nakedness made Sheree sit up straighter, open her eyes wider.

Who were these beautiful men?

Just by looking at them, she judged that their dance would be wildly sensual, perhaps even bestial.

She shivered at the final thought. She'd heard and seen many things since arriving in New Orleans, but she knew men could be bestial no matter whether they lived in the city or the countryside.

Anything Goes

The men, their legs wide apart, knees bent, bowed stiffly as if they'd been carved from stone.

Open-mouthed, Sheree watched every move they made, fascinated by their very shininess in the enforced gloom of the club.

She saw them reach for something from their belts. Suddenly, their eyes peered through slits in ornate ceremonial masks of red, yellow and bright blue.

They were hideous masks, and yet, at the same time, they were oddly intriguing and pleasantly frightening.

The lone wail of some kind of pipe or flute suddenly drifted into the room.

The men began to dance, their knees always bent, their lower bodies seeming to remain stiff whilst their upper bodies writhed and swayed to the sound of the haunting music and, as it seemed to Sheree, the pounding of her own heart.

Her breath caught in her throat when she saw them take knives from their belts. They were huge things that flashed in the light of the lone candle on their table and the moonlight that came in via a fanlight above a thick wooden door.

The dancers whirled, their knives held high, the haunting music sending shivers creeping down Sheree's back.

She felt Rene edge nearer, but could not look at him. She was spellbound, lost in some primeval time slip that drew her to it.

Just when she thought the dance had reached its climax, a slim, crying girl was dragged out onto the floor by another man.

Her wrists were tied in front of her, and her head fell forward, then rolled, and fell backwards as she cried out in a language Sheree did not understand. And yet, it didn't matter that she didn't understand the language. She knew from the girl's actions and her heartfelt pleas that she was crying for mercy, and the way she was crying sent icy shivers down Sheree's spine.

The girl was flung to her knees, then the man who held the rope that fastened her wrists pulled it backwards so that she lay back with her legs bent beneath her.

Her breasts were bare except for a small cloth that hung from a neck collar. One of the masked dancers pulled it back so it fell over the girl's face.

Legs still wide, the men stood either side of her, their knives raised high.

Sheree covered her face with her hands, but peered through the gaps in her fingers.

The two dancers brought the knives down slowly and circled them over the girl's breasts.

Sheree heard the sound of whimpering. Her whole body now felt icy cold. Should she rush to stop this? *Of course not, you fool. This isn't real. It's just entertainment.*

The haziness caused by the champagne had dissipated completely. This tableau, whether it was real or not, was absolutely riveting and, despite her terror, she didn't want to miss a thing.

A small piece of fabric was all that covered the girl's abdomen. One of the masked men bent down and, with his knife, severed it from the red belt around her waist.

Sheree knew that Rene was watching her as she gasped her surprise. The girl's sex was completely hairless, a shining brown slice of flesh with a width of pinkness running through its middle.

Sheree moved to the edge of her seat as one of the men began to sway and chant a strange, throbbing song that sounded full of evil intent, although she did not understand a single word.

He held his knife so that the blade faced downwards and slowly, so very slowly, he began to bend his knees more until his haunches were close to the ground.

A sacrifice! That surely was his intent.

As this terrible realisation grabbed hold of her. Sheree grabbed at Rene's arm.

'Please, Rene! You must stop it!'

Her eyes pleaded with him. Her face was flushed with fear and her mouth hung open.

'Please!'

Rene merely smiled at her, then tapped on her arm and pointed to what was now happening.

When she turned her gaze back to the tableau, she saw that the man had laid both his dagger and his gold-edged apron to one side. He was now between the girl's legs, seams and dents appearing in his well-muscled buttocks as he thrust himself in and out of the moaning girl.

As he plunged his penis into her, he clasped both her thighs tight against him.

Her hips were higher than her head. Her body sloped backwards and her arms were still stretched out beyond her head.

Up until now, the other masked man stood like a statue, his blade held downwards in front of his face, his knees bent, his legs far apart so that the gap below formed half of a square.

But, as Sheree watched him, he straddled the girl's head, then went down on his knees.

With a quick movement, he removed his gold-edged apron and placed it to one side. He put the knife on top of it.

Sheree could not tear her eyes away from the scene. The girl was still whimpering, but differently now. Here and there she cried out as the man between her thighs quickened his stroke and lunged into her more deeply.

In a way, Sheree felt she had been duped by the scene. She had been through the whole gambit of terror and fear for the girl. She had truly thought the girl would be killed, instead of which the only thing she was sacrificing was her sex.

The second man now squatted over the girl's face, his balls coming to no more than an inch above her mouth. Suddenly, he reached behind him with one hand and put his other hand on her chin.

Puzzled, Sheree looked on, then flushed slightly when she realised what he'd done.

By pinching the girl's nose and getting a grip on her chin, he had forced her to open her mouth. As she did so, his balls slid in and, as he began to rock to and fro over her, he pulled on his penis.

It was a while before he tired of this but, when he did, he got on to all fours, his penis hanging over the girl's mouth before she accepted it.

The sound of the men's chanting and the high wail of the Pan pipes helped those watching to suspend belief.

Mesmerised to the very end, Sheree still could not quite believe it when all three men and the girl got to their feet, smiling widely behind their masks.

All four bowed. Rene clapped. Sheree stared after them as they left the room.

Rene came closer. His arm encircled her shoulders and

his lips kissed then licked at her ear.

'Did you enjoy the entertainment I provided for you, *ma Sheree*?'

'I can't believe . . .' Sheree placed a hand on her breast – as if that would stop her heart from thudding like it did. 'I thought that they were going to . . .'

'Kill her?'

He stroked her hair as he said it, then wove delicious circles among the fine hairs at the nape of her neck.

'Ye . . .ss. I did . . . I thought . . .'

Sheree could not stop herself from stammering.

She took her head vigorously as if to shake off the strange emotions she was feeling.

'I was terrified, and then I was . . .'

'Aroused?'

Rene had thrown in the word so casually. And yet she knew that deep down there was nothing casual about it. The scene and her reaction had all been calculated. But what for, she asked herself? What for?

Seemingly, Rene answered the question for her.

'Our agreement is signed. Tomorrow I will take you to my home. There you will discover your own terror. Your own sensuality.'

Sheree stared at him.

'I don't understand.'

Not once had that confident smile left his face.

He touched her cheek and rubbed gently at a place where some make-up might have smudged as she'd watched the dancers.

'You will, *ma chérie*. You most certainly will.'

Chapter 17

Rene Brabonne enjoyed driving, though he wasn't too keen on the journey he was undertaking this fine spring day.

He'd travelled this way many times before and for the same reasons. What was eating him, for God's sake?

But he put a brave face on things and smiled at his passenger. Each time he did so, an accompanying throb occurred in his loins which resulted in an inelegant lump appearing at the front of his trousers.

For her part, the green-eyed, coffee-skinned girl who had been called Shirley Anne before she arrived in New Orleans, sat doing her best not to look disappointed.

Rene had not made any move to seduce her the night before. Why was that? Surely he must have noticed she wanted him to. The entertainment he had put on for her had inflamed her body. What effect had it had on him? This, she decided, was the moment to ask him.

'Last night's floor show – it was very . . .' She fumbled for the right word. 'Different.'

Rene kept his eyes on the road ahead. 'Different? In what way?'

Sheree was a little peeved that her question had been answered with a question.

'I really thought they were going to kill her. She was a sacrifice, wasn't she? And the knives were real weren't they?'

She looked at him, saw a muscle twitch in his cheek; knew he would have to answer.

A faint, slow smile creased his face then was gone.

'And then?'

Sheree felt suddenly embarrassed. He wanted her to describe what happened. Did that turn him on, just talking about it? She recalled the thoughts she had read from both his and Stacey's mind. He liked watching, so maybe he liked having sex described to him too.

She took a deep breath and folded her hands in her lap like some child about to explain why they had done so miserably at school.

'They didn't stab her. At least, not with a knife. I hadn't expected that. I really thought . . .'

'That they would kill her because you saw their aggression . . .'

'And felt her fear . . .' Sheree blurted.

Rene's smile returned and he shook his head, his hands sliding round the wheel as they took a sharp bend.

'Why did you think she was frightened?'

Sheree didn't hesitate. 'Because she trembled and she whimpered when they tore her clothes from her. And she couldn't save herself. She was frightened. I know she was. I saw her shiver, I heard her cry out.'

Rene shook his head again, an action which made Sheree frown and feel suddenly angry.

'Ma chérie. Has it not occurred to you that there is a very fine line between fear and pleasure. They are bedmates. Anticipation of either causes trembling and moans of pain or delight. What you saw last night proved that.'

Sheree narrowed her eyes and shook her head. 'I don't understand.'

At the very moment she shook her head as if to clear her mind, there was a sudden burst of activity from the side of the road. The view through the windscreen was blotted out by a blanket of billowing whiteness. The tyres squealed, the car swerved as Rene slammed on the brakes so quickly that the engine stalled and they came to an immediate stop.

Heart thudding, Sheree followed the blanket of whiteness that had so suddenly come upon them.

Two pelicans, their feathers glistening in the sunlight, flapped their wings and soared higher, loose feathers trailing behind them and floating down onto the road and the car bonnet as they rose into the sky.

Sheree watched them soar, her heart no longer thudding and her sudden fear turned to instant wonder.

She was only vaguely aware of Rene restarting the engine.

'You see, Sheree. Your own fear turned to wonder. Just like the girl last night.'

His words lingered with her as they drove. She still wanted to ask him why he hadn't made the effort to seduce her, but was too proud to ask. After all, she knew from reading both his and Stacey's mind that their sex life was far more adventurous than Mr and Mrs Average America.

So an odd silence hung between them. Sometimes Sheree's thoughts returned to the pagan scene that had started by terrifying her and had ended up arousing her. On top of that she wondered exactly why she was going to the Brabonne Plantation. Rene had told her that his mother would like to meet her. He took all his favourite girls there, and no doubt Sheree herself would find the family history of great interest. It didn't seem a very good excuse, but she was obliged to go along with it.

'What if I don't want to come with you?' she'd asked petulantly. 'Isn't it up country a little where the mosquitos outnumber the people?'

'Use lemon juice to deter them,' he replied. 'Besides, if you read the small print of the contract you signed last night, you are obliged to do almost anything I ask.'

She was going to ask him if sex was included in the contract and could she back out of it if he failed to uphold his side of the bargain, but he didn't look in the mood for sassy questions. He continued to keep his eyes on the road. Whilst he did so, Sheree took advantage of the fact. She studied his classic profile, his high cheekbones, well-formed eyebrows and swept-back dark hair. His looks sent a shiver through her and, for the very first time, she realised that shiver was partly fear, partly desire.

How would it be, she wondered? His body against hers. His hand pressing her buttock so that her body fitted tightly against him and his erection prodded her belly demanding she open the gates and let him in.

For his part, Rene wasn't looking forward to this trip as much as he had to similar ones he had carried out with young women who were just as beautiful as his latest songstress. It would have dented his ego somewhat to admit that he would have preferred to keep this one to himself. Deep down, he knew it was the truth. But tradition demanded he submit to the will of his ancestors.

So stop looking at her, he told himself. *If you keep glancing at her like that, she will smile like she does, then you will have to pull over to the side of the road and take her here and now. That means you would have spoiled the merchandise, and Mother would not be pleased with you.*

So Rene made an extra effort to keep his eyes on the road while Sheree gazed unseeing at the scenery.

Despite the roads from New Orleans having been upgraded in recent years with the coming of the automobile, their condition deteriorated once they'd gained the rich countryside around the Mississippi delta where mules hadn't entirely been superseded by the tractor.

Rene narrowed his eyes as he drove and did his best to divert his mind from the young woman sat beside him. Because of what was about to happen, his thoughts automatically went to his wife.

Stacey had been peeved as usual when he'd told her where he was going. He'd asked her to accompany him, but she'd declined.

'And wilt beneath your mother's contemptuous gaze. Not me, Rene darling. I'd sooner wilt in the heat of this damned city. And, anyway, it's her world. Her show.'

Rene had not been entirely disappointed that his wife would not be accompanying him. He smiled as he glanced appreciably at the slim form beside him so elegantly turned out in a bright yellow shift and a matching hat with navy trim and similar shoes. He could hear the rustle of her silk stockings as her knees rubbed against each other. Just thinking like that, he began to imagine the way her stocking enclosed her leg and how her garter formed a barrier between the covered flesh of her leg and the white, naked flesh of her upper thighs.

He took a deep breath of air, but in his mind he was sniffing the warmer confines up under her skirt. He was imagining the feel of her flesh beneath his hands and the smell of her once he had coaxed her legs open.

In his mind his fingers were sliding over her inner thighs and sliding beneath the crutch of her silky soft knickers to her silky soft pubic hair.

Tight curls, he thought. Tight, black curls that spring around the fingers. And warm, slippery, sensual flesh that moistens the fingertips and swells in response to gentle manipulation.

Perhaps, he thought, the moment might come yet. If he could lay his sense of duty aside, he would have her in exactly the way he wanted to have her. But tradition . . .

No. He mustn't think like that. He must remember what she represented; what he represented. Best if he'd never set eyes on her. But he had, and doing so could be his undoing.

From the first moment he'd seen her, he'd contemplated her body, but only whist in the company of his wife.

But he had fallen for Sheree. He knew it and Stacey knew it.

'Get her to sign that contract, Rene,' Stacey had insisted. 'It's time for her to go.'

He had deliberated. He admitted that. But now it was done and there was no turning back. Sheree and her contract would be up to the highest bidder and, so far, she knew nothing about this. But she soon would. Once they were at his family home, he would put her at ease by showing her round the place. After that, his mother would take charge of

Anything Goes

her and, following in a long line of historical precedents, she would get her ready for the main event.

He tried to convince himself that everything would go smoothly; that Sheree would not kick up a fuss at being sold along with her contract.

He thought of the others who had gone the same way. Others like Emmeline who had gone on to dance at the famous Cotton Club.

There were no guarantees that everything would run smoothly. His mother ran a strict house and Sheree might be a little surprised at some of her eccentricities. Not that those eccentricities were part of her character, but more an inherent family tradition.

What would be Sheree's response, he wondered.

He took the opportunity to glance at her. He smiled at her reassuringly before turning his eyes back to the road. It wasn't easy to concentrate, and the vision of her naked thighs and the feel of her sex beneath its covering of silk didn't help.

His thigh rubbed gently against hers, which in turn ignited a delicious tingling in his crotch. *Say something*, he thought to himself. *If you say something, you'll regain your self-control*.

'Nearly there.' It was all he could manage as the red dust that gathered between road and gutter swirled up then resettled as they passed.

She merely smiled. He wondered what she was thinking. Had Stacey told her of the family business and how a humble bunch of Canucks had ended up owning such a fine house and land? He hoped not. Not yet. It might frighten her away.

Chapter 18

Errol made a few enquiries at big houses where servants were changed as often as bed linen, but didn't get very far until he reached the last one.

It was a cream painted house with green and yellow sun-blinds pulled out over the windows, the same sort he'd seen used over the windows of ice-cream parlours.

He'd got no reply at the front door, so went round to the back and knocked on a pale green door that looked in need of painting.

A slim, big-eyed girl with her black, woolly hair tied back in a stiff bun beneath a starched white cap opened the door about six inches, looked him up and down, then opened it wide.

He asked her whether Shirley Anne had come asking for a job.

'Can't say I remember the name. What sort of job would she have been after?'

Errol shrugged. 'Hell. I don't know. Maid, I suppose. Something like that.'

The girl he was talking to pursed her lips. There was a lot of daring in her eyes and a sassy tilt to the way she held her chin. 'Was she pretty?'

She raised one eyebrow suggestively whilst she studied him from head to toe.

Errol nodded. 'Yes. Green eyes. Dark brown hair. Slim. Nice figure. Like yourself.'

She smiled. 'Thanks, big boy.'

Errol felt like blushing. It wasn't that anyone hadn't called him that before, it was just that this saucy piece of skirt had glanced suggestively at his cock as she said it, and his cock responded as though taking it personally.

Sweat erupted at the nape of his neck and began a slow, sexy trickle down his spine.

The girl seemed to notice he was getting uptight. 'You feeling hot?' she asked him. 'Like a lemonade here in the cool?'

As she asked, she jerked her head in the direction of the cool from behind her.

Although he had certain reservations, Errol nodded. Yes, he was thirsty. Yes, he was hot. But the last time he'd gone into a grand house, he'd been treated to a lot more than a glass of cool lemonade.

'It's freshly made,' the girl said as Errol followed her into a stone-slabbed room which looked as if it were used for storing anything that needed to be kept cool.

Hams, smoked to a deep ginger, hung from iron hooks set into a white painted wooden ceiling. A truckle of cheese from which wedges had already been cut sat on a bench along with a churn of milk, a mountain of bright yellow butter and three basins of eggs.

The mix of smells was like a range of curtains hanging in the air. Walk near the hams, it was their smell that floated up his nose. Walk next to the cheese, it was that.

Errol's stomach rumbled in anticipation that he might yet get more than mere lemonade. Food of this quality wasn't obtainable in some of the cheap joints he'd been eating in.

The sound of a bolt being pulled across a door made him jump suddenly.

'Hey,' he said, hands up, palms outwards as he backed away from the girl and in the direction of the door through which he had entered. 'I don't like being locked in. You hear?'

The girl tilted her head to one side like she had before and folded her arms. Her look was disdainful.

'I was going to give you some food as well as some lemonade. Do you think I want to lose my job? If anyone comes through that door there, I sure will. So do you want to eat or what?'

Errol thought for a moment. The door behind him was still unlocked. The door across which she had slid the bolt was behind her and obviously led into the rest of the house.

He nodded. 'I want to eat, and some of that lemonade of yours will go down well.'

'Hm!' She tossed her head, then put two big tumblers on the table. After that, she fetched a big stone jug.

Errol licked his bottom lip as the cool-looking liquid poured from one receptacle to the other. The smell of lemons hung gently in the air.

He reached for the lemonade.

'Sit down,' the girl said. 'I'll slice you off some ham and some cheese.'

As he drained the last of the lemonade, she slid the plate of ham, cheese, butter and thick crusty bread under his nose. Errol breathed in the smell of the food before attacking it. Once his teeth were embedded in the cheese, the girl refilled his tumbler.

'So what's your girl's name again?' she asked.

'Shirley Anne,' he replied after swallowing enough to allow him to speak.

'And what's yours?' she added.

'Errol,' he managed to say.

As he wiped his mouth with the back of his hand, his eyes met hers. She was staring at him, but smiling as she did so. There was some hint of intent in her eyes and Errol was jolted into sudden reality. What would she want in return for the drink and the food? There had to be a catch somewhere.

'My name's Lacey Lee,' she said suddenly. 'Kind-hearted sort, I am. Wouldn't you say so?'

He nodded and drained some more of the lemonade.

'Can't help you with looking for your girl, though. I'm afraid the food will have to be enough for you.'

He murmured his thanks, buried his mouth and eyes in his lemonade again and began to think about leaving.

'Of course,' she went on. 'There is a price.'

He looked across at her and caught his breath. She was smiling and stroking her neck. But it wasn't that he was looking at.

Lacey Lee had unbuttoned the front of her dress. Her small, brown breasts were resting on the table, the nipples almost as big as saucers and staring straight at him.

The chair Errol had been sitting on fell backwards as he jumped to his feet.

'I have to go!' he blurted.

'You can't,' she said smiling. 'Not yet. Not until you've paid me for what you ate and what you drank.'

His experiences with Amber still fresh in his mind, Errol stared at her. He suddenly remembered the money he had in his pocket and began to rummage.

'Here,' he said pulling out a few dollars and thrusting them at her.

Lacey Lee continued to smile.

'It's not money I want.'

'Look,' Errol blurted nervously. 'I got to find Shirley Anne. I don't want to linger round here. No, sir! No way!'

Lacey Lee continued to smile.

'I'll tell you where she is – if you give me what I want.'

Errol was halfway to the door when she said that. He stopped in his tracks. The hand that reached for the door handle stopped as if frozen, then fell to his side.

'You know where she is?'

Smiling, Lacey Lee nodded. There was a look of triumph in her eyes.

'The master was going to give her a job. He'd have given her a lot more too, given half the chance. But my mistress stepped in. She didn't exactly read his mind, but she sure knew a rival when she saw one. There was no way that girl was getting a job in this house or any other around here.'

'So where did she go?'

Lacey Lee cupped her breasts and let them rest on the table whilst she used her fingers and thumbs to stroke her nipples to greater prominence.

Errol let his eyes fall on what she was offering him. Would it matter if he complied with what she wanted? After all, who would know about it?

Let yourself go.

His body immediately complied.

Her breasts were shiny, her nipples dark as tamarind seeds. *They'd feel nice*, he concluded. The thought took root in his mind, and his groin. His penis stirred and hardened.

He went behind Lacey Lee. He paused, took a deep breath then, like a diver, he plunged in.

She moaned and lay her head back against his belly as his hands kneaded her neck and her shoulders. She closed her eyes. He cupped her face in his hands, bent over, kissed her forehead, her nose, lips and chin. As he did this, his hands cruised down over her breasts until his fingers were on her nipples.

Immediately he had touched the fatal hardness of her nipples, his cock filled with blood and desire.

Her breasts were soft as silk, yet firm with youth. At first her nipples were tight and hard like pecan nuts but, with his assistance, they grew until they resembled the corks he'd pulled from ginger-beer bottles.

He pulled at her nipples almost cruelly as he used them to lift her breasts from off the table.

She cried out, a thin, wailing sound that arced between being a sob of pain and a cry of delight.

The sound pleased him. It was like a salve to the way he had been treated by the red-haired, white-fleshed Amber.

Revenge made him calculating. Lacey Lee was using him. Not as Amber had used him. He was not chained up and made the subject of perverted games, but she was still forcing him to do this. Not that it wasn't pleasant. Lacey

Anything Goes

Lee was a pretty girl and one he wouldn't have passed by in ordinary circumstances.

But things were no longer ordinary and, in his mind, he began calculating just how he wanted to use her.

First, he pulled her to her feet and forced her to lie across the table, her breasts squashed against the rough wood of what was obviously used as a chopping block.

Then he hoisted her skirt up to her waist.

As he unbuttoned his trousers, he surveyed the thin white fabric that covered her plump bottom. Plain black garters held up her black, wool stockings. Between them and her knickers, the backs of her thighs were as shiny and dark as the buttocks that strained against her underwear.

Errol hooked his fingers in her knickers and wound the crutch round tightly so that it almost disappeared into the crack of her bottom and the cleft between her legs.

'Oow, use me,' groaned Lacey Lee.

It was then it occurred to him that rough treatment was Lacey Lee's pleasure. In effect, she was the opposite of Amber. She was the one who wanted to be cruelly used. He was the one who must use her.

Something of the memory of what he had been through, coupled with the sight of Lacey Lee's bottom and the smell of her sex, made him want to do all that he could to her.

Close to his face, a carving knife had been left embedded in the joint of ham. Errol took hold of it. Tugging the screwed up underwear away from Lacey Lee's body, he sliced the knife through the thin material so that the crutch fell away. He hacked at the rest of the material until that too fell from her body.

'Oh, more!' he heard Lacey Lee cry, her big brown

bottom wriggling and now exposed fully to his view.

He threw the knife to one side. The sight of the girl's naked buttocks was too much to resist. He placed his palms on them and began to knead them in big, firm circles, pushing them inwards, then pulling them outwards at which point he could gaze at the small daisy of a hole that nestled in between.

'Please,' he heard the girl murmur. 'Please . . .'

But he didn't want it to end. Not just yet.

Instinctively, he knew she didn't want it to end either. He eyed her shiny-skinned buttocks. They quivered slightly, and suddenly he knew he wanted them to quiver more.

He raised his hand, then brought it down to land with a loud thwack.

'Oh! No!'

The cheeks of her bottom quivered, then tightened. The sight of it responding that way made Errol pause for a moment. Then his cock, which was now free of his trousers, jumped with excitement.

Errol landed another loud slap on her bottom. Then another.

Each time the richly coloured flesh rippled, then firmed up.

'Stop doing that,' Errol cried, his hand landing on her behind yet again. 'Stop tightening up. Stay loose. I want you to stay loose!'

'Whatever you want me to do. Whatever. Anything at all.'

Errol could hardly believe his ears. His heart was already thudding in his chest. Never could he have imagined that revenge could taste so sweet.

Hearing her words made him think of how Amber had

tied him up and told him he would do whatever she wanted him to do. Thinking of her voice ordering him like that made him decide what he wanted to do to Lacey Lee.

He glanced at the shredded knickers, then up at the hooks from which the cured hams were hanging.

The pieces of shredded underwear were quickly picked up from the floor.

'That's right,' he exclaimed. 'You will do whatever I want.'

He tied the pieces of fabric around her wrists but left a loop in the middle.

He pulled Lacey Lee to her feet then, lifting her up, he looped the fabric that tied her wrists together over one of the empty hooks that hung from the ceiling.

Arms stretched high above her head, only Lacey Lee's toes reached the floor. She looked at him from between her arms, her eyes full of a strange kind of fear.

Aware that his penis was thrust out before him like a drum-major's baton, Errol wondered whether the sight of it frightened her.

Then he realised it wasn't fear at all. It was anticipation. Lacey Lee was wondering what he was going to do next.

There she hung, her dress hiding her body.

The dress. Errol decided it had to go.

He looked round him to see where the knife had landed. Once it was in his grasp, he slashed at her dress and her underwear so that it fell in pieces from her body.

'Oh my!' she cried. 'My dress. It's ruined! What are you going to do to me? What are you going to do?'

This, Errol knew, was all part of the acting. She was enjoying this, savouring the trepidation of not knowing what he would do next.

The throb in his groin was so powerful that he could feel its echo in his ears. Sexual desire had replaced the blood in his body. It flowed through his veins like hot, molten lava, newly excreted from a deep, hot volcano.

His brows lowered over his eyes as if to better direct his gaze.

He took in the sleek brownness of her body, the gleam of her skin. Her breasts seemed to quiver. Her belly tightened and, as it did so, the clutch of pubic hair that sat like a tangled powder puff at the top of her legs seemed more luxuriant, more enticing.

His eyes were drawn to the whole of that beautiful area around her hips and thighs. Perhaps it was because of the fact that she was still wearing her plain black stockings and garters. There was always something extra arousing about being part undressed rather than completely naked.

Tremors of passion made the muscles of his arms tense and bulge shiny and proud against his skin. He stepped towards her and looked deeply into her eyes. Her mouth hung slightly open.

He towered over her, his shadow dominating hers. Then he kissed her, his fingers holding her jaw roughly so she could not turn away until he allowed it. When he did so, she was breathless, her whole body pulsating with both her need and his.

'Oh, please,' she mewed, and he knew she meant for him to do more.

The shadows in the cool, stone-slabbed room grew longer as he began to slide down her body, his fingers pulling on her nipples until his mouth got there.

Her skin was like velvet beneath his lips. Her nipples

sweet as cherries in his mouth.

When he got to her belly, he poked his tongue into her navel and tasted her saltiness, the sheer femininity of the flavour of her flesh.

Running his hands down her back and onto her buttocks, he buried his face in her crotch, sucked in her smell and her taste, the curls sweeping over his tongue and tangling in his teeth.

As the tip of his tongue slid between her pubic lips and tapped gently on her clitoris, his hands covered the fullness of her bottom, his fingers probing the gap between.

Her response was electrifying. Errol felt her whole body tense like a coiled-up spring, her muscles taut, her ribs straining against her skin. He heard her cry with delight.

When he straightened up, he kissed her again and transferred the taste of her sex onto her lips. Her tongue came up to take it. Her lips sucked on it, relishing her own taste and the sheer delicacy of the operation.

Then, as the taste was transferred, he gripped her buttocks, then slid his hands along her thighs, lifting her so he could best put himself into her.

She offered no resistance. Her legs rose, clamping around his waist, her ankles crossed there.

He pulled her buttocks towards him as the head of his member parted the moist frills of flesh that gathered round her vagina like the petals of an exotic flower.

He heaved, thrust himself forward until half his length was in. Another thrust, and his whole length was in her.

'It's too big,' she mewed, and made Errol feel proud.

He knew he was full swollen. Knew he was a big guy anyway. But to hear some woman say it was unbeatable.

Spurred on by her comment, he rammed himself tightly against her so that her opening was entirely sealed with the width and the length of him.

Errol felt a tight bunching of muscles and an incurable ache running along his penis. His release was not far off, yet he was adamant that Lacey Lee would climax first.

Like most women he'd known, he knew she would appreciate short, quick little movements that would put the most pressure possible on her clitoris.

Buttocks bunching, he jerked his pelvis backwards and forwards in quick bursts, his pelvic bone slamming firmly against the place where it really mattered.

He instantly knew he'd taken the right action when she threw her head back and thrust her breasts towards his face.

Arching her back, she cried out.

Errol calculated the precise moment when her climax had reached its apex and caught hold of her nipple with his teeth. He tugged at it, sucked it right into his mouth and, just as he had expected, she screamed – but not with pain. It was a kind of exhilaration, like a whoop of triumph coming from someone who had achieved what she wanted. And she had done just that.

He felt her legs tighten around him, squeezing the breath from his body as she enjoyed the full pressure of his flesh against the full length of her vulva.

Trembling like her body, her voice gushed out unintelligible sounds that were more like a tune than mere words.

In his mind he could almost feel what she was feeling. It was as if she had wound something up deep inside herself and that something was connected to him. Because of that feeling, the climax she was experiencing transferred to him.

Like her he spasmed, threw his head back and let the sensations of pure release wash over him.

His mouth opened. Arteries and veins became full of blood and strained against the thin flesh of his throat.

His stomach muscles tightened. His buttocks did the same because he was finalising the last few thrusts that would lodge his semen within her vagina.

When the final thrust came and his emission spurted into her, his cry of triumph was not dissimilar to hers.

At the end of it, each received what they truly wanted. Lacey Lee had been fucked by a big man with the sort of body normally seen only on classic Greek statues. Errol, for his part, got the name of the club where Shirley Anne had got a job.

Chapter 19

Six white pillars supported an Athenian style portico in front of the Brabonne house.

It was not quite what Sheree had expected. After all, Rene freely admitted his Cajun roots, but had not admitted to the fact that, unlike most of the Canadian French who had fled from British rule, his family owned such a palatial abode.

Sheree, smelling of perfume and lemon juice, got out of the car and, with leisurely, graceful movements, smoothed her skirt down over her hips, then adjusted her hat.

She glanced quickly at Rene.

'Please,' he said politely and, with a flamboyant gesture, indicated that she follow him.

The door that opened on their approach was of well-polished wood with a handle of brass that was as bright as sunshine.

'Good morning, Master Brabonne.'

The woman who opened the door had skin the colour of demerara sugar, eyes as dark as bitter chocolate, and white fluffy hair that framed her face like a cluster of summer clouds.

'Your mother is in the drawing room.'

Sheree noticed the woman glance at her almost appraisingly before she turned her back and led them across a polished wooden floor on which thick Persian-style rugs were thrown.

At the very moment they stood before the door to the drawing room, Rene came to a halt and held his arm out to bar her way. Her nose banged against it as she came to an abrupt halt.

'Rene—' she began.

He turned to her. 'Be quiet.' His tone was more clipped and superior than she had ever heard it before. 'You will wait here. My mother will want to see me alone. She may want to meet you, or she may not. Mame will take care of you for now.'

He did not wait for a response from either her or the full-bosomed servant, but merely shoved his hat and cane at the woman he had addressed as Mame. She took it without comment or being thanked as Rene turned quickly on his heel and opened the door that had been so resolutely barred to her.

A shaft of light and the smell of lavender spilled out of the drawing-room door before it closed behind Rene Brabonne.

Sheree stared after him, then took a deep breath and tried not to look nervous.

'If you take a seat, I'll bring you some tea.' Mame's voice was as dark as her skin. Sheree looked up at her and smiled.

'That would be nice.'

'But I have to service madam and the young master first before I get yours.' She sounded as if it was a duty to be performed within a strictly allocated time, almost, thought Sheree, as if she'd been punished if some unspoken rule wasn't strictly adhered to.

'Fine.'

Sheree did a very good job of looking unconcerned. She sat down in a well-stuffed sofa that had scrolled ends and cabriole legs. She felt a tingling deep inside that she couldn't really account for. It was as if something was about to happen that would heap demands on the more sensual side of her nature. What form it would take, she didn't know.

The door closed behind the retreating servant and Sheree took advantage of being alone to look round.

Deep crimson paper lined the high-walled hall. The ceiling was high and raftered and the floor was of black and white tiles laid in the Dutch pattern and relieved only by the addition of thick red and blue Turkish rugs.

There was an obvious opulence about the place, but there was also something a little disconcerting.

The sofa was soft beneath her bottom, the rugs thick beneath her feet. She was alone, yet felt she was being observed.

High on the walls, hanging from brass chains fixed in even higher, were gilt-framed paintings of men and women who bore a striking resemblance to the man she had arrived with.

She eyed the well-shaped thighs of those that wore breeches, the barrel chests of those that wore trousers, and the creamy white breasts of the female members of the family who displayed their decolletage so proudly. Something about the look in their eyes made her shiver. What was it? There was no cruelty in their gaze. No haughtiness about the tilt of their head or the jutting of their chins. There was just a calm all knowingness about their expressions, and a certain lasciviousness in their eyes. It was as if the long-dead eyes were assessing her value or seeing through her smart suit to the lace-trimmed underwear beneath.

'Here is your tea, miss.'

Mame's voice made her start. She tugged her gaze away from the figures in the paintings.

'Thank you.'

As the tea was being poured, she noticed that Mame gave her curious glances.

'Is something wrong?'

Mame looked quickly away, dipping the tongs into the sugar and missing the lumps on the first two occasions.

'Nothing wrong, miss.'

The ideal servant. Sheree thought to herself. Mame, she judged, was the sort that noticed everything but said nothing. And yet, Sheree was convinced there was some meaning in her look. She decided on a different tack. Gain her confidence. Get her talking about other things, things that seemed completely innocuous.

'These portraits.' She nodded at the men and women who gazed down at them from different paintings and a different age. 'Are they all family members?'

Mame's dark eyes moved to where Sheree was looking.

'They sure are.'

'What are their names?'

'Names? Well. Let me see.'

Mame's eyes seemed to search for a place to start. She pointed to a middle-aged woman with a heart-shaped face and pink cheeks. Auburn hair sat in a pile on top of her head and coiled over each ear. It may well have been Sheree's fancy, but she was sure the woman's nipples were peeping over the top of her dress like the pink eyes of two plump, shy pigeons.

'That is Mistress Yolande Brabonne. She was a Miss Cartwright from Savannah before she married. And that one,' she went on, her long, brown finger pointing to another woman who wore a high empire line dress and had fair ringlets falling around her face, 'is Mistress Lydie Brabonne. She was a la Roquette before she married.'

Her breasts too, Sheree noticed, were displayed quite unashamedly.

'And the men,' Sheree interrupted. 'Who is that man there?'

She pointed to a tall, dark figure whose painted eyes seemed to be scrutinising her more intently than any of the others.

'That is Master Robert Brabonne.' She pronounced Robert in the French way, the 't' nonexistent. 'He was married to Clarice. That's her over there.'

She pointed to a grey-haired woman with a pinched expression dressed in a crinoline of 1840's vintage.

'She looks older than him.'

'She was. She was an heiress. Brought a lot of money to the marriage.'

'And children?'

Mame gave her a confused look.

'Master Robert had many children.'

She began to bustle about the finished tea things, her hands and fingers flying to fit everything back onto the tray.

'But *she* didn't,' Sheree said softly.

Mame paused. Her eyes met Sheree's. 'He was a red-blooded man. All the Brabonnes were like that. Marriage to them was no different than signing a contract for anything else. She brought her money to the marriage. He brought his land and his status. Both families were pleased with the match. Both had a high standing in society.'

The door to the drawing room opened just as Sheree thought of a few more questions she would like answered. But the opportunity had passed.

Rene, shoulders back, his silhouette sharply defined against the brightness of the room he was exiting, smiled as he approached her.

A tall, graceful woman, grey hair stretched firmly away from her face, followed behind him. She was dressed in a pale mauve dress of a very soft material that swirled around her lean form as she moved.

'This is Sheree,' Rene explained to his mother as he introduced her to Sheree. 'I named her myself.'

Sheree held out her hand. It stayed there, alone in mid-air. Madame Brabonne did not even appear to notice or, if she did, preferred to ignore it.

She held her head high, and there was a disdainful look about her mouth. The cold, white sparkle of top-quality diamonds flashed in her ears.

Sheree tensed. Was it her imagination, or was Rene's mother regarding her as if she were a piece of prize bloodstock or a farmyard cow?

Her worst suspicions were confirmed when Madame Brabonne began to comment on her as though she wasn't really there at all.

'What an enchanting creature. Where did you find her?'
'She arrived at the club. She was looking for a job.'
'Lucky for you. I think that out of all the mixed-blood women I've ever seen, she is by far the most dramatic. Quite exceptional. I think she would have made quite a splash in Robert's day.' Again the French pronunciation.

Sheree stood as if dumbstruck. She wanted to respond, to say something really notable. But she couldn't. Rene had warned her to mind what she said and to be obedient.

Madame Brabonne's gaze slid sidelong to her son.

'She would have been a worthy concubine in the family tradition. I trust you have already broken her in to that particular pastime. I trust your wife approved.'

Sheree's calm expression began turning into a glower.

'Excuse me!'

Madame Brabonne gave her son a knowing look.

'Fiery with it. Just as you predicted.'

Sheree's mouth dropped open. She was speechless, and yet she was also intrigued. What was at the root of this odd conversation?

As if aware that she was seething fit to burst, Madame Brabonne suddenly turned to her.

'It doesn't really matter whether Stacey approves or not, of course. As long as tradition is honoured. She is a good representative of all that was best about the family, this plantation and this house.'

Sheree was lost. She wanted to shout some sort of defiance, and yet she wasn't entirely sure what she would be protesting about.

Regal as a queen, Madame Brabonne, the woman in mauve, glided into the middle of the room. She turned round, face uplifted, eyes surveying the paintings of all those who had gone before.

'Scions of a dynasty,' she exclaimed as she stood before the woman in the empire line gown. 'They came here, you know, with two sons and two dozen female slaves. They were the only slaves they ever bought. They bred their own after that.'

Sheree blushed as Madame Brabonne's eyes met hers. There was almost a look of triumph in them as if she were daring Sheree to think the very worst.

'Women slaves are less trouble. The male children were always sold off.'

Sheree did not voice the thought that came into her mind. Was this woman saying what she thought she was saying? The women slaves had reproduced, but only females had been kept, the male children being sold off. And the sires of those children? The answer was obvious. Each member of the Brabonne family had married and even had children. But as Mame had said, the family married for dynastic purposes, not for love or pleasure.

The female slaves had been the harem of the Brabonne men, and over a period of time the slaves' skins had lightened.

Sheree glanced again at some of the eyes staring down at her from the paintings. She fixed her gaze on Robert Brabonne. He stared back at her. It was then that she realised that his eyes were as green as hers.

The older woman chuckled, obviously delighted to see Sheree's reaction.

'They got paler of course. But then, that's not exactly a bad thing is it. And, anyway, this was like one happy family.'

Anything Goes

Sheree's throat was suddenly very dry. She should have been outraged, but she wasn't. Instead, she felt excited by such a revelation, and in turn felt guilty that such a confession should make her feel that way.

It was Rene who saved the day.

'Come,' he said taking hold of her arm. 'Let me take you around my family home.'

Sheree went silently, disinclined to voice any of the thoughts in her mind lest she offend.

He took her to the stables first where a pair of chestnut horses were stabled next to a pair of dapple greys.

'Despite my trying to persuade her to buy an automobile, my mother insists on keeping her horses. Part of her past, she says. I cannot change her mind.'

A jumble of thoughts still racing round her mind, Sheree patted each of the velvet-soft noses that nuzzled at the fine linen of her dress. She had to broach the subject.

'Am I getting the picture, Rene?'

She looked at him almost accusingly, and yet she knew he would see a certain excitement in her eyes.

A slow smile spread across Rene's face. His blue eyes twinkled and she could almost believe the whole thing had been put on purely for her benefit.

'In the early part of the last century, this place was nothing like any other plantation. It was like one great commune. One giant family.'

Sheree shook her head disbelievingly. 'But what of their wives?'

'They did not object. Things were different then, *mon enfant*. A marriage was a contract. Business was business.'

Confused more than shocked, Sheree turned away from

him, but he took her elbow and guided her down a red-brick path that led away from the stables and into a courtyard that had a lawn in the middle and a bird table made from the same red bricks as the path.

'The women's quarters,' he said quietly.

A strange chill ran down Sheree's spine as she eyed the arched doorways and the blue painted window frames of the single-storey cottages.

'Would you like to look in?' Rene asked her.

Sheree shivered. She had a compulsion to say no, to turn and stomp away. But she also had a desire to stay, to look and to wonder how those women had felt submitting to a man and a family who owned them body and soul.

'Come,' Rene said, his hand again on her elbow.

The cottage he took her into was very cool compared to the glaring heat of the courtyard outside.

There was a large fireplace and pretty furniture. A mass of wild flowers sat in a vase on the table as though someone had just placed them there that morning.

Mame, Sheree thought.

A window at the back of the cottage faced the grass and trees that sloped off down to the river.

Sheree stared out at the scene. Even before Rene actually touched her, she knew he was going to.

His touch was gentle on her shoulders. His thumbs began to work at the sudden tenseness that had seized her neck. She moaned, closed her eyes and rested her head against his lips.

'This,' he whispered, his breath mingling with her hair, 'was a house of pleasure. Just like the Catnip Club in a way.'

'But how can you . . .?'

Her stomach tightened as she half turned round to face him. Her words were lost as his lips covered hers. What she had wanted, and what he had wanted had at last happened.

All her strength seemed to leave her for a moment. His arms encircled her, drew her close. His chest pressed hard against hers, crushing her breasts back against her ribs.

She tried to draw away.

'Sheree,' he whispered. 'Please. Be grateful. You are my star. The most beautiful attraction the Catnip Club has had in a long time.'

'Your wife . . .?'

He smiled as he shook his head. 'A contract. A business arrangement. For both of us.'

Deep down, Sheree knew that this man had got under her skin. She also knew that she needed to be grateful to him. But she was wary of throwing her chances away by virtue of a jealous wife. Stacey catered for Rene's sexual foibles, but she would not tolerate any emotional involvement. Sex only. That was it.

'Do you expect me to believe that?' Her voice was trembling.

'Ask her. Ask her about her lovers. She will tell you there is nothing to fear. Truly.'

Sheree needed a man. She knew that. Other women needed new clothes, children, or even gin to give that extra zest to their lives. She needed a man, and Rene, with his twinkling blue eyes, gleaming black hair and hybrid accent definitely did something for her.

'I am grateful,' she managed to say.

His eyes held hers. 'Then prove it.'

'How?'

He smiled and took hold of her hand. He tapped at her lips as he might those of a small child.

'I will show you. Come.'

Chapter 20

It was midday and the sun had found chinks in the wooden blinds that shielded the Catnip Club from the brightness of daylight.

Dust motes swam in a sea of yellow light that seemed as out of place in the club as a pack of Jesuit priests.

Max raised his horn and pursed his lips. He took a deep breath and his cheeks became bloated with air.

There was a jaunty joy to the tune he played and, as it thumped out of the brass, his foot tapped the floor.

Because the tune was happy and he was happy, he got lost in the racy notes and the swiftly changing scales.

It wasn't until he could actually smell her perfume, that he realised Stacey was standing beside him.

Closing his eyes, he went on playing.

Stacey persisted.

The club disappeared as she lifted her skirt and let it fall over his head. He immediately stopped playing.

'Stacey!'

'You're ignoring me.' She sounded petulant.

Max glanced up at her. She looked annoyed. He noticed she was holding a piece of paper in her hand.

Max sighed as he took the mouthpiece away from his lips.

'I've things on my mind.'

He started to raise the trumpet once more.

'So have I,' Stacey growled. 'This,' she hissed as she waved the piece of paper. 'This is on my mind!'

Max got to his feet.

'Look, Stacey, I really don't want to know . . .'

Stacey glared. 'I know, Max. I filled a gap. Or rather you filled mine!'

She laughed after she said it. As though it were the funniest thing in the world. Max merely grimaced.

'Look,' he said, placing his trumpet inside its velvet-lined case and clicking it shut. 'I've got other things to attend to, Stacey. I'm off from this place. I've got to meet someone.'

Stacey looked shocked.

'I didn't know you were leaving.'

Max raised his eyebrows but tried not to look her straight in the eyes. He had trouble saying 'no' to Stacey. She had a way of getting the best of him that was similar to Emmeline. Powerful women, he thought. Both of them.

He nodded in answer to her question. 'I'm off to pastures new, Stacey. I'm meeting Emmeline from off the train.'

Stacey stared.

'Emmeline? But I thought her contract was . . .'

'Yes. For two years.' Max interrupted brusquely. 'When we understood it was only for one. Rene lied. You lied. Lucky some Englishman took pity on her. Paid off her contract.' His eyes blazed.

Stacey looked uncomfortable as though she were thinking fast and trying to find a way out of her current embarrassment.

'I can't believe it. The Cotton Club don't usually let go that easily.'

Max merely shrugged her aside and started to make his way to the door where a green exit light flickered uncertainly above it.

'Not my problem.'

'No,' Stacey murmured. 'It's mine.'

Suddenly, she grabbed Max's arm. 'Look, Max. I'm sorry, but I have to tell you. It's about to happen all over again. Rene has got Sheree to sign a similar contract to Emmeline, only this one is to a man from Berlin who has just opened a nightclub in Paris.'

Max looked bemused.

'So what? Won't you be glad to get rid of her? All of us could see that Rene was a bit more fond of her than he should have been.'

Immediately after he'd said it, Max knew he'd hit the bull's-eye. Stacey looked furious.

'Rene has always wanted to go to Paris. There's an appendix to the contract saying that Rene can go to Paris as Sheree's manager.'

Max eyed her a little coldly. Stacey was manipulative, more of a controller, in fact, than his darling Emmeline. Today, for the first time, he'd seen fear in her eyes. Fear of losing Rene to another woman. A sudden thought occurred to him.

'And how much does Sheree know about this?'

For a moment, Stacey held his gaze. 'I doubt if she knows anything at all.'

'Excuse me.'

They both turned to where a good-looking guy dressed in

dark green trousers, a white vest and a black jacket had entered.

Stacey did a double take and, liking what she saw, turned round to face him.

'I'd excuse you anything,' she purred, her eyes scanning his six-feet-four-inch frame.

'I'm looking for someone,' he said. 'I've been told she's been working here. Her name's Shirley Anne. Do you know her?'

Max, who up until now had been more interested in taking his instrument and getting out of the place, suddenly brightened.

'Dark hair, coffee complexion and emerald eyes?'

Eyes as dark as bitter chocolate and face like burnished bronze cracked into an instant smile.

'Sounds like her. Have you seen her? Have you?'

Low and husky as his voice had been, it seemed to go higher with the expectation that he had fought what he'd been looking for.

'Only we have a problem,' said Max, and quickly grabbed the contract from Stacey. 'Someone's got her to sign a contract that will take her out of the country and perhaps tie her to a guy she might not want to be with. Might make her do things she doesn't want to do either.'

Errol's happy face darkened. 'And who might that be?'

Max glanced at Stacey who suddenly looked a lot more optimistic than she had done.

'Come with me, and you'll find out. But first, I have to pick someone up from the station. She's the best person to fill you in on the details.'

Chapter 21

Rene led Sheree away from the pretty cottage, out into the sunlit courtyard, then back into the stables which were cool because they were built of stone and whitewashed inside.

The horses shifted in their stalls and looked expectantly over their shoulders as he led her into a barn at the end. There was a tack room to one side where bridles, saddles and carriage harness sat in neat racks. On the other was a grain store and the hay barn was straight on.

'I love the smells in here,' he said as he led her into the barn which was strewn with dark yellow straw. More straw bales were stacked in four by six squares for easy access and, further along, hay was stacked in the same way.

'Straw. Hay. Fresh leather.' Rene took a deep breath between each word.

He took off his jacket and turned to face her. The look on his face was different than it usually was. Their eyes met and, in that instant, she knew exactly what was going to happen. She also knew why it had never happened so far. Back in New Orleans he would have had to include Stacey. Out here he didn't need to do that. Out here, on his family plantation, he would have her all to himself.

Mouth smiling, eyes sparkling, he stepped towards her. Sheree became very aware of his smell. *I love the smell of men*, she thought to herself, and immediately there was a tingling in her breasts and a low kind of throbbing throughout the length of her vulva.

Breathing more quickly, she watched as Rene began slowly to take off his shirt.

'You cannot believe how long I've waited for this moment,' he said as he undid the starched collar and cuffs of his expensively tailored shirt. 'Alone. At last.'

Sheree's breath caught in her throat. 'Yes.' The word came out sounding similar to a leaf rustling in a breeze, lower than usual. Husky. Warm.

There were no more words she wanted to say. Her body was on fire for his, and her own movements, her very words, seemed too ungainly for a time such as this.

Rene was every inch the southern gentleman, the type who never stank of stale sweat or unlaundered clothes. Creamy soap had washed his body and cologne enhanced the natural smells he already owned.

She had an urge to run her hangs along his shoulders and run her fingers through the frills of dark hair that covered his chest.

I've never done that with Errol, she thought to herself. Errol, whose chest was shiny, smooth and brown. The contours of Rene's body were pleasing, but his muscles were not as developed as Errol's. His skin was paler too. In comparison, Rene resembled a well-bred gentleman's hack. Errol was more like a sturdy young stallion, rippling with well-defined muscles where arteries and veins stood proud beneath his skin.

Anything Goes

To Sheree's surprise, Rene no longer filled her senses as he had done. It had been a while since she'd thought of Errol, and now he had popped back into her mind and lodged there as if he had never left.

Sexual arousal no longer seemed to be the result of the man standing before her, but of the man in her mind.

But did it matter which man had aroused her?

She decided it didn't. She also decided she would enjoy taking a fiendish delight in thinking about Errol whilst making love with Rene.

He didn't order her to take off her dress, but she did anyway. Carefully, she placed the neat navy and yellow outfit on a bale of hay and laid her underwear with it too.

Soon, she wore only her shiny silk stockings and a pretty pair of garters. The fresh air on her body felt good and she responded to it all by herself, wetting her finger and running it round her nipples as if to prepare them for what was to come.

Rene's eyes raked her body and, as he looked, her nipples hardened and her stomach tensed. He might just as well have been touching her.

'Lie down,' he ordered and pointed at a pile of hay in the corner.

Sheree tingled at the sound of his voice. Her whole body seemed to erupt in goose bumps. Not because she was cold, but because what was happening in her mind and what was happening in reality sent her blood racing with passion.

In her mind, she remembered being in the straw with Errol and him taking her from behind as she looked out of the barn window and passed the time of day with two middle-aged women who'd just come out of the church opposite.

With that in her mind, she did as Rene asked, then watched as he removed his clothes before coming to her, his penis swaying before him, of a good size but perhaps not so big as that of her darling Errol.

Desire overrode any other feelings she might have had towards Rene Brabonne. Her breath seemed to stall in her throat as her eyes swept over his well-shaped body and lingered on the erect rod that thrust like an unsheathed weapon from beneath his thighs.

His warmth seemed to reach her before his body did, like a cloud of warm rain rides before the sun. He knelt beside her. A droplet of fluid glistening on the end of his rod caught her eye. A dryness came to her throat along with an urging for her tongue to take the droplet from off his cock.

She trembled as he reached for her, his palms covering her breasts. His hands were warm and she welcomed them, stretching so that her back arched and her flesh forced itself into the warmth of his hands.

A sense of abandonment washed over her and she closed her eyes. There was no need to see this man, to know who he was. His touch, the tone of his voice was enough.

The smell of hay, straw and leather mixed with that of his body and his desire. She closed her eyes and murmured sweet words, though he could not know they were not for him. They were for Errol and were the words she had used on that day when they'd made love in the hay loft and the two women had kept her talking.

She'd wanted to cry out in ecstasy. She'd wanted to murmur words that were both exceedingly passionate and appallingly lascivious. But she had restrained herself. And as Errol's cock had pumped its cargo into her, she'd merely laughed throatily and agreed with the women that it was indeed a lovely day for a ride in an automobile, or even behind a horse and cart.

'A good day for any sort of ride,' she'd cried out, and the women had nodded, astonished at her enthusiasm for such a suggestion.

Her body undulated at the thought of the sweet scene and the feel of Errol's hard cock cleaving her sexual lips asunder, ramming into her body, his balls slapping rhythmically against the back of her thighs.

Again and again, she went over the same scene in her mind; Errol fucking her. Errol coming. The women's expressions. It all added to what she was feeling.

She moaned as Rene's hands ran down over the flatness of her belly and tickled the concave dip just before the rising of her mons.

Soon, she thought as she opened her legs slightly, *he will put himself into me. Soon I will be in ecstasy*. She also knew that whatever he did, in her mind it would be Errol doing it. Errol, who knew so many ways and so many places in which they could indulge in their wildest fantasies.

Errol, whose sexuality was completely natural. Whose body was so strong, so firm, and whose sexual thrust was as powerful as the pistons that drove the latest Henry Ford car.

'Turn over,' Rene said suddenly, his voice hot with desire.

He pushed her over onto her belly, then slid his arm beneath her and hoisted her up onto her elbows and knees. She moaned with ecstasy and wriggled her bottom invitingly as his fingers played with her pubic hair then slid between her sexual lips.

Delirious with pleasure, she cried out for more as his finger invaded her inner lips. It didn't stop there, but travelled on to tap and touch her clitoris until it swelled with passion and danced with excitement, raising its soft, pink head and hardening beneath his demanding touch.

She squirmed on his finger, raising her hips, offering her body to him, tilting her backside until it wasn't far from his face.

It was his for the taking. She was fast falling among her own sensations, growing dizzy with her own desire and not really caring how he had her and who was around when he did.

Even the two middle-aged women, she thought. Any audience would do.

Suddenly, she could control herself no longer. She was ready for him. Her wetness was seeping from her, running down the insides of her legs and dampening the straw on which she lay.

'Fuck me,' she demanded. 'Please!'

Her cry was almost desperate. And that was exactly how she felt; desperate for something more vigorous, more substantial than a finger to be inside her.

His inspection of her private parts seemed to falter. She heard him sigh, felt his hands fall away from her.

He sighed, a long mournful note, full of sadness.

She opened her eyes, fully expecting her gaze to meet the stiff penis she had seen earlier. The sight that met her eyes was not expected.

His erection was lessening. His hands were hanging at

his sides and a regretful expression was on his face.

Sheree raised herself onto her hands, the spikiness of the straw scratching at her arms. She frowned.

'What's the matter?'

He shook his head and spread his arms disconsolately. His eyes, like hers, were on his cock.

'I think it's dead,' he said.

Sheree raised her eyebrows. 'Dead? I don't understand.'

Rene shook his head again. 'I thought I could manage it all by myself. But I can't. My cock is a creature of habit. In fact, it seems at times to almost have a mind of its own.'

'Rene, you are talking in riddles. Do you want to do me or don't you?'

'I apologise, Sheree.' His look matched his voice. 'But this is the way things are. I cannot perform unless I attend to certain matters first. As I said, it is a matter of habit. I thought both I and my penis had grown out of such things. Obviously, I was mistaken. At least as far as my cock is concerned.'

Sheree controlled the sudden urge to laugh. What this man was saying was funny. And yet, at the same time, it was sad. So was his face.

Gently, she stroked his arm and kissed his shoulder.

'Rene. Please don't take on like this. Surely we can do something about this can't we?'

He nodded. 'Yes. Or rather you can.'

Puzzled, she tilted her head sideways, her eyes betraying her need to know.

'Like what?'

He reached just above her head and scraped some straw

away. A metal ring hung in the wall. Two leather thongs hung from it.

'Would you . . .?'

So powerful were the mental images of what her and Errol had done in the barn, that without him needing to say anything more, Sheree lay back in the straw and raised her arms above her head.

Rene smiled. 'Thank you.'

Not another word passed between them as Rene wound the soft leather around her wrists and tied it securely.

A knot of apprehension tightened her stomach muscles. She felt fear, but she also felt excitement.

I'm like the girl that was sacrificed, she thought to herself. *I'm like her, lying there naked, waiting for the weapon to slice into my body*.

Like the girl, the weapon that would slice into her body would be an erect penis.

No sacrifice, she told herself. More a silent submission.

'That's better,' he said, his eyes shining.

Sheree's gaze went to his penis which had now shot upright, immediately reattaining its earlier proportion.

He bent down, spread her legs, and bound her ankles to two more iron rings that were set into the close-fitting flagstone floor.

Her whole body ached for him to mount her. She writhed among the straw, moaning low and huskily. She arched her back and thrust her breasts upwards like two creamy hills topped with dark, red rock.

'Please,' she murmured, her eyes imploring him, her voice full of pleading. 'Please.'

She had fully expected him to take her, to kneel between

her legs, then lay himself over her and push his shaft into her entrance.

To her great astonishment, he did no such thing.

All signs of sexual desire had left his face. Not even a smile remained. It was as though he had been summer and now winter had arrived.

'Rene?'

He turned away from her and bent to his clothes.

'Rene?'

Now there was panic in Sheree's voice. She began to fight against her bonds. There was panic in her eyes. This was not going the way it should be going, at least, not as far as she was concerned.

Rene, his penis now shrunk to a more manageable size, was putting on his clothes. He did not look at her as he did so.

'Rene. What is it? Aren't you going to do it to me?'

'Of course he's not, my dear.'

Sheree started as she recognised the voice.

Rene stepped to one side as a figure with grey hair and wearing a mauve dress took his place.

Madame Brabonne now really did study Sheree as though she were no more than a piece of livestock. A cow or a horse perhaps. Even a sheep.

'Rene's intention was just to get you into the mood. He already knows you are a creature of bestial appetite. He has watched you pleasure yourself in that apartment you lived in. Judging by that alone, we know you are exactly right to carry on the tradition of the house of Brabonne, a tradition I insist upon.'

Wide-eyed, Sheree looked at her without understanding.

Madame Brabonne looked to her son and then back at Sheree.

'As my son has already explained to you, through generation after generation we bred our own slaves in this place. Alas, of course, it is no longer allowed. But my son humours me. Perhaps after my death the tradition will die. But whilst I continue, the tradition will continue.'

'What tradition?' Sheree, face gaunt with fear, looked quickly from mother to son and back again. 'What tradition?'

Suddenly, she saw again the tableau Rene had put on to entertain her. Had she been mistaken? Was it really a rehearsal for what was to happen to her? Would she really be sacrificed?

True terror made her body shake and her lower lip tremble as she attempted to ask a question.

'Are you going to kill me?'

Madame Brabonne stared at her for what seemed like minutes. Then she blinked.

'Kill you? Of course not. We're going to sell you. I've just told you, you stupid girl. We bred slaves. You have signed a contract to sing and do . . .' She paused as though not savouring what she had to say next. 'Other things. Things men like women do on demand. Your contract, my dear, is being sold on. Tonight, many men are coming to attend the bidding. Most of them have already heard you sing. Now they will want a sample of your other "skills". And you my dear, will oblige. In fact, you can hardly refuse.'

'You can't! Please! You can't!'

But Madame Brabonne had already turned away. Her next comment was directed at her son.

'Come, Rene. Let us go back to the house. Our guests will

not be here until three this afternoon. Mame has prepared the food and drink. It should really be a night to remember. I'm looking forward to it immensely, aren't you?'

Sheree heard him answer his mother as they turned to leave.

'No,' Sheree cried. 'You can't do this!'

Madame Brabonne turned round.

Immediately she faced her, Sheree became terribly aware of her embarrassing predicament. She struggled against her bonds, desperately trying to close her legs so Rene's mother could not gaze on the glistening pink flesh all ready for Rene, or any other man, to take advantage of. But that, she realised, was exactly what all this had been about. Rene had been arousing her, making her juicy and ready for what was to come.

'You signed a contract, girl. You cannot go back on it now. Do you want to read it through again?'

Eyes fixed on Sheree's face, Madame Brabonne clicked her fingers at her son.

'I've got it here somewhere.'

He immediately began rummaging in his jacket pockets.

His mother held her pose, fingers not too far from his face.

Shamefaced, he stopped searching his jacket and looked directly at her. 'I don't appear to have it with me.'

Madame Brabonne gave him a disparaging look as her arm dropped to her side. 'That could be very difficult. A potential buyer might not be inclined to wait until you post it to him.'

Rene glanced between her and his mother.

'I'm sorry,' he said and, somehow, Sheree knew that his apology was for her as much as for his mother.

Chapter 22

Stacey's car was very flashy and very fast.

Even so, Errol was finding the journey overly long. He was frantic to see Shirley Anne again even if she had changed her name to Sheree for stage purposes.

'Step on that gas,' he exclaimed, his eyes narrowed against the dust thrown up by the secondary road they travelled along.

'We'd better have a plan of action,' Max stated, his voice half muffled by the wind.

'What makes you think we need one?' Errol countered.

Emmeline, the flimsy material of her skirt stirred by the breeze to reveal her stocking tops, intervened. Errol averted his eyes, but listened.

'Because the buyers are going to be pretty put out at having their fun curtailed. Knowing Rene, he's really got Sheree – sorry – Shirley Anne in the mood for hot sex. And those guys attending Madam Brabonne's little soiree are going to be hot as a Texas bull in the mating season. And they're going to be plenty angry if they don't get what they want.'

Max gave Emmeline a sidelong glance.

'But *you* coped.'

She smiled at him and tapped his nose with her finger.

'But that's me, Maxie baby. I can cope with anybody. You know that, honey bun.'

Although she caught the hasty glower Stacey Brabonne threw her via the car's rear-view mirror, Emmeline still smiled, her eyes gazing straight ahead.

When they got to the Brabonne place, there were a number of cars parked outside.

Emmeline raced up the steps and pushed at the big front door. It opened, just as she had expected it to. Mame was right behind it.

'I saw you coming up the steps,' she explained, her attention firmly fixed on the bubbling Emmeline.

'I'm glad you did, Mame.' The others, who had followed Emmeline in, stood round as the vivacious younger woman pecked the older one on the cheek.

'Have they already gone over?'

Mame nodded. 'Not too long ago, so the bidding won't have started yet.'

'Good!' Emmeline turned to the others. 'Who's got the contract?'

Max took it from his inside pocket. 'I have.'

'Right. Then let's be getting there.'

It was Emmeline who led the way rather than the wife of the man who had organised all this. Max glanced back at her wondering why she seemed so reluctant to face her husband.

Of course it was embarrassing to find out that he intended shoving off to France without her. But he sensed there was more to this than Stacey was letting on.

When they got into the barn, a group of men and one woman stood with their backs towards them.

Errol shifted himself round to the side so he could better see what was going on.

When he saw what was happening, an uncharacteristic fury came to his face.

Two men were knelt down either side of his darling Shirley Anne. Both were fondling her breasts with one hand whilst their other hand played with her sex.

Shirley Anne's head was thrown back. Unable to escape their arousing manipulations, she was groaning, and her back was arched, her whole body tense with uncontrollable reactions.

Someone clapped suddenly.

'So easily aroused. How exquisite. How splendid!'

The man who spoke had a decidedly upper-crust English accent.

'She responds like a fiddle does to the bow,' commented another man with a German accent. 'I am determined that the contract shall be mine. This lady will grace my latest salon in Paris. Vienna is too vulgar for anything too exotic or, indeed, erotic.'

He chuckled and a few others chuckled with him.

Errol had seen enough. He stepped forward.

'Shirley Anne isn't going anywhere except home!'

He leapt to where the girl he loved lay. Floored by a clenched fist, one of the men at her side went flying. The other stood up, froze, then smiled icily as he reached inside his jacket.

The butt of a gun appeared, but the man did not have time to draw it out further.

Max delivered a hefty rabbit punch to the nape of the man's neck.

Emmeline, then Stacey followed her into the ring.

Voices of those who had come to bid were raised in anger. For a moment, there was a lot of shouting from both sides. Then one voice broke through it all.

'Quiet! All of you! I will not have my peace shattered by the baying wolves or the bleating of sheep!'

They all turned to look at Madame Brabonne. Even Errol, who was attempting to undo Shirley Anne's bonds, looked up at her.

'You!' She pointed at Errol. 'And you!' She pointed at Max. 'You do not understand what you have done. You have broken a tradition that has lasted nearly two hundred years. It was a flame we kept burning. A symbol of our own independence. This auction must go on.'

'Shirley Anne is coming home,' Errol shouted.

Madame Brabonne raised her eyebrows in a haughty manner as she addressed the would-be rescuer.

'It is her choice. Along with the contract she would have had fame and fortune. And in return she would have only been doing things she likes doing. Or is this a nun we have here?'

Errol looked down at Shirley Anne. 'Do you want to go to Paris?'

Shirley Anne, or Sheree as she'd become accustomed to being called, raised her head. 'Paris. Is that where I'm supposed to be going?'

'If my bid is acceptable,' said the man with the German accent. 'My latest nightclub is situated just off the main thoroughfare in Pigalle.'

'And that would have been it,' broke in Madame Brabonne. 'She would have gone there for two years, and Rene and I would have carried on as before.'

'Oh no you wouldn't!'

Now it was Stacey's turn. Her face was screwed up with anger as she faced the woman she hated most in all the world.

'Your darling son was leaving.'

'Leaving you?' The look she gave her daughter-in-law was filled with contempt. 'So he should. As I said to him, he should never have married you in the first place.'

'No!' Stacey exclaimed. 'He's not just leaving me. He's leaving you as well. He has made plans to go to Paris as that girl's manager.' As her mother-in-law was suitably taken aback, Stacey turned to her husband. 'Yes. Rene. I know what you're up to. You've fallen for that girl. You were off with her. I know all about it.'

Rene too looked taken aback. He opened his mouth as though he were going to make an attempt at explanation. Then he closed it again and, covering his eyes with one hand, he turned away.

Stacey grabbed the contract from Max. 'As for this . . .'

Rip went the paper. Again and again, she bent it, folded it, and tore it into tiny pieces. Then she threw the whole lot up in the air and it fell to the ground like heavy snow.

Chapter 23

'I don't suppose we could do a private deal?' asked the last of the party who had attended the bidding.

Errol exchanged a glance with Shirley Anne, then shook his head.

The man concerned took one last look at the naked girl who was still spread-eagled among the straw. Noticing the barely repressed fury in Errol's eyes, he then turned swiftly away to follow the others up to the house.

As moonlight replaced sunlight and began to throw silver light through an opening high up the barn, Errol bent and kissed her lips.

Because she did not respond to him with as much passion as he had expected, he pushed himself back up onto his arms and looked down at her.

'You wanted to go to Paris, didn't you?'

He saw the sudden secretive look on her face. She nodded.

Errol sat up and looked away from her.

'You can g if you like. I won't stand in your way.'

There was a silence that followed and stabbed him like a knife. Why didn't she deny she wanted to go there? Why didn't she say she wanted to stay with him?

He looked over his shoulder at her.

Her breasts rose provocatively as she sighed and looked back at him.

'I wanted to see what life outside the bayous was like. That's all it was, Errol. It certainly wasn't because I didn't love you, 'cos I do.'

Errol turned away again. He felt hurt and it would have been easy to be angry. But he couldn't be. At least, not with her.

It was hard making the decision. It was even harder telling her.

He lay on his side beside her and rested his head in his hand.

'What if we renegotiate a private contract with that guy that wants you to sing in his nightclub in Paris.' He held up one finger. 'Sing only mind, Shirley Anne. No sex. Not with him anyway.'

He figured it was a fair proposal. He wouldn't be telling her about Amber and Lacey Lee. Fearfully, he waited for her response.

A broad smile crossed over Shirley Anne's face.

'Can we do that?'

A slow smile passed across his face.

'We can do anything we like.'

As small creatures fluttered overhead or scurried through the straw, Errol began caressing Shirley Anne's body.

He didn't bother releasing her from her bonds and she didn't protest about him not untying her.

Just as she had done with the men who had fondled her, she arched her back, threw back her head and closed her eyes as Errol sucked on her teats and fingered her pussy.

In a way, she felt she was flying. Familiar sensations were flowing like quicksilver through her body. But there were also other things.

Life, she decided, was indeed an excitement. It was something to be feasted upon. No act of sensual delight could be determined as sinful. If it was enjoyed, then it was OK as far as she was concerned.

As Errol's lips trailed down over her stomach, she imagined that it was one of those men doing it as the others watched.

Now she could understand just why Rene was turned on by watching others. Watching or being watched, there was little difference. It was like attending a performance at a theatre or a movie house. Actors and audience were both enjoying what was happening. That was the way it was. That was how nature had intended.

He took her there amongst the straw, the weight and strength of his body warming her naked flesh.

Behind her closed eyelids, Shirley Anne thought about all that had happened and all that would happen. But her ambition and yearning for better things was swamped by the sudden rush of desire that flushed through her body.

Had she really missed Errol that much?

She realised she had. He was something that had always been there. Something she would always be part of no matter where they were and who they were with. And that was good.

Chapter 24

Max set Emmeline's bells ringing.

He hadn't been able to wait until they got back to New Orleans and Emmeline, being Emmeline, had been just as infused with sexual hunger as he had.

Stacey seemed to be having one hell of a row with her husband and mother-in-law, and the latter was also rowing with her son.

Emmeline took full advantage of the situation by lifting the car keys from Stacey's purse.

Next to a grove of willow that shot like arrows from the side of the rod, Emmeline got out of the car and stripped off.

Max's eyes lit up with delight as he again espied the range of pretty little bells that decorated Emmeline's body.

'Now my turn,' Emmeline had cried once she'd decided he had played with the bells long enough.

She began to dance for him, the bells jingling and ringing as she kicked up her legs, shook her breasts, then leaned backwards into a crab so he could better see the single bell that hung from her swollen clitoris.

The dance got wilder and wilder until at last she was

breathless and her eyes were bright with desire.

'You've got to fuck me now,' she stated. 'I want it like this.'

She leaned over the luggage carrier at the rear of the car and slipped her wrists beneath the straps that usually held luggage in place.

'Fuck me now,' she cried in the most pitiful voice he'd ever heard her use. 'Please. Fuck me now!'

He couldn't believe his ears. Not because of Emmeline's ripe language, but because of her imploring him to take her.

In the past, it had always been Emmeline who called the shots. What, he wondered, had happened to change her?

Fly buttons open in no time, he came to her and groaned with delight as he felt the bell she had in her clitoris pass pleasantly over his penis.

Blood rushed to his head and his penis more quickly and fiercely than he had ever known. Strange sensations of wanting to be completely in her – body, legs and even linen jacket – engulfed him. He wanted all of himself in her.

But he settled for what was in her. Throbbing and spitting the first globules of semen, his cock swelled to make a close fit in the receptacle it found itself.

As he relished the feel of her vagina contracting on his member, he played with her nipples, ringing the little bells and having a yearning to kiss them, suck them, and trace with his tongue the pale blue veins he could see in her breasts.

The bells seemed to play a tune for them when they came, both locked together, body against body.

Afterwards, once he had slid out of her and his hardness had all but receded, he asked her about the Cotton Club.

'It was good,' she said brightly, then took hold of his arm. 'But I still missed you.'

Max looked suddenly embarrassed. 'It must have been nice, though, to dance at a swell place like that.'

'Oh, it was nothing.'

Max took hold of her by the shoulders, shook her slightly and looked into her eyes.

'It wasn't just nothing. It was really something. I'd dance with the devil if I could perform in a place like that.'

Emmeline stared at him.

'It means that much to you?'

Max was not the most forthcoming of guys, but this time he was resolute.

'It means one helluva lot to me!'

A thoughtful look crossed Emmeline's face.

'How about if we see what's available elsewhere. Just for a change.'

'Even if for only a little while?'

Emmeline nodded. 'We'll give it a try.'

Chapter 25

Rene looked panic-stricken and Stacey relished the fact.

'Choose!' she shouted. 'Your mother or me!'

Rene's usually straight shoulders seemed to stoop.

He really doesn't know what to do, thought Stacey. *Well, hell, I've had enough. This is the end of the line.*

'Her?' Madame Brabonne looked her daughter-in-law up and down as if she were a warped old apple tree that needed pruning. 'What have you brought to this family? Peasant bloodstock?'

Furious, Stacey glared at the woman who had hated her on sight merely for marrying her son.

'Honesty!' she shouted. Then she realised what she had said and how truthful it was. 'Honesty,' she repeated. 'Your son has needs, Madame Brabonne, and I have taken care of those needs. I have pimped for him...' She paused as she saw the startled look on her mother-in-law's face. She smiled. 'That's right. You did hear correctly. I pimped for him. Isn't that what peasant stock's supposed to do? Meet the demands of their betters?'

Madame Brabonne's face turned to thunder.

'No, No. No.' Rene crumpled into a chair, his head in his hands.

'How dare you!'

Stacey stood firm and folded her arms.

'Of course I dare. I dare because deep down I'm better than you. My family never kept slaves to do everything for them. They never married for money and treated sex as a commodity rather than a pleasure. Your son, Madame Brabonne, whether you like it or not, responds to what I do for him. I get him the girls he wants. I pleasure him whilst he watches them pleasuring themselves. In short, I am indeed his pimp and his pimp I will stay. He needs me.'

Madame Brabonne stood shocked, her mouth hanging open. She at last found her voice and turned directly to her son.

'Rene, you must put this woman aside! She is trash. Just southern white trash!'

'Rene.' Stacey held out her hand to her husband. 'Rene,' she repeated again. 'I am your wife. You appreciate everything I do for you. You know you do. Now, come with me. Forget your family and everything that's past. Forget Paris. Come with me and I will procure for you just as I did before.'

Rene rubbed his hands over his face and stared at the floor.

For a moment, a look of doubt crossed Stacey's face.

'Rene. We have a show to put on tonight. Your star is gone. We must find a replacement.'

At last he looked up at her, but he didn't look the man he had been. He looked crushed.

He glanced at his mother, then swiftly looked away.

Once he did that, Stacey knew she had won.

Rene got shakily to his feet. His mother reached for him. He backed away.

'I have to go, Mother. I have a nightclub to run.'

Stacey smiled at him as his hand slipped into hers.

'Come on,' she said alluringly. 'We've got our own history to make.'

Epilogue

Montmartre had no rules, no scruples, and little in the way of morals. Eighteenth-century buildings of yellow, pink and cream that were caught on canvas by a man named Utrillo were the homes of those seeking *laissez-faire* and self-expression.

The apartment Errol and his wife shared was on the first floor and had a balcony on which Sheree grew bright red geraniums in terracotta pots.

Max and Emmeline had an apartment on the ground floor which had double glass doors that led out onto a small patio where white star-shaped flowers grew out between the warm amber-tinted tiles.

It was seven in the morning and the sun was rising when all four of them went out onto the patio, the two men carrying a bottle of good burgundy each, and the women carrying wine glasses, Camembert, Brie and fresh crusty bread.

They sat at a green slatted table with unmatched chairs.

Max looked wistfully out through the foliage that hid their world from that outside.

'You know, I never really appreciated New Orleans until

I came here. It's as though the old Latin Quarter back home is a bit like one of them geranium cuttings you girls are always messing with. It got cut off. Got transplanted, and then just grew.'

'But you are glad you came here, aren't you, honey?'

Emmeline covered his hand with hers and looked up into his eyes.

He looked at her and smiled.

'Why shouldn't I be? Richthof pays me well to play at his club and there's no strings attached.' He nodded at Shirley Anne who had now changed her name permanently to Sheree. 'And our little girl there has the city at her feet. So have you with that Salome-style dance of yours.'

Sheree caressed Errol's neck.

'What about you, honey? Do you miss New Orleans?'

A distant look came to Errol's eyes. Thoughts of the town on Le Farge and the woman with white flesh and red hair came to his mind. So did his sojourn with the outrageous Lacey Lee.

He shrugged as he smiled.

'Paris and New Orleans are like twins parted at birth. But they've both basically got the same roots. With either of 'em it's a case of anything goes. And it does!'

A Message from the Publisher

Headline Liaison is a new concept in erotic fiction: a list of books designed for the reading pleasure of both men and women, to be read alone – or together with your lover. As such, we would be most interested to hear from our readers.

Did you read the book with your partner? Did it fire your imagination? Did it turn you on – or off? Did you like the story, the characters, the setting? What did you think of the cover presentation? In short, what's your opinion? If you care to offer it, please write to:

> The Editor
> Headline Liaison
> 338 Euston Road
> London NW1 3BH

Or maybe you think you could do better if you wrote an erotic novel yourself. We are always on the lookout for new authors. If you'd like to try your hand at writing a book for possible inclusion in the Liaison list, here are our basic guidelines: We are looking for novels of approximately 80,000 words in which the erotic content should aim to please both men and women and should not describe illegal sexual activity (pedophilia, for example). The novel should contain sympathetic and interesting characters, pace, atmosphere and an intriguing plotline.

If you'd like to have a go, please submit to the Editor a sample of at least 10,000 words, clearly typed on one side of the paper only, together with a short resume of the storyline. Should you wish your material returned to you please include a stamped addressed envelope. If we like it sufficiently, we will offer you a contract for publication.

More Erotic Fiction from Headline Liaison

SEVEN DAYS

Adult Fiction for Lovers

J J Duke

Erica's arms were spread apart and she pulled against the silk bonds – not because she wanted to escape but to savour the experience. As the silk bit into her wrists, a surge of pure pleasure shot through her, so intense that the darkness behind the blindfold turned crimson . . .

Erica is not exactly an innocent abroad. On the other hand, she's never been in New York before. This trip could make or break her career in the fashion business. It could also free her from the inhibitions that prevent her exploring her sensual needs.

She has a week for her work commitments – and a week to take her pleasure in the world's wildest city. Now's her chance to make her most daring dreams come true. She's on a voyage of erotic discovery and she doesn't care if things get a little crazy. After all, it can only last seven days . . .

0 7472 5094 4

If you enjoyed this book here is a selection of other bestselling Adult Fiction titles from Headline Liaison

PLEASE TEASE ME	Rebecca Ambrose	£5.99
A PRIVATE EDUCATION	Carol Anderson	£5.99
IMPULSE	Kay Cavendish	£5.99
TRUE COLOURS	Lucinda Chester	£5.99
CHANGE PARTNERS	Cathryn Cooper	£5.99
SEDUCTION	Cathryn Cooper	£5.99
THE WAYS OF A WOMAN	J J Duke	£5.99
FORTUNE'S TIDE	Cheryl Mildenhall	£5.99
INTIMATE DISCLOSURES	Cheryl Mildenhall	£5.99
ISLAND IN THE SUN	Susan Sebastian	£5.99

Headline books are available at your local bookshop or newsagent. Alternatively, books can be ordered direct from the publisher. Just tick the titles you want and fill in the form below. Prices and availability subject to change without notice.

Buy four books from the selection above and get free postage and packaging and delivery within 48 hours. Just send a cheque or postal order made payable to Bookpoint Ltd to the value of the total cover price of the four books. Alternatively, if you wish to buy fewer than four books the following postage and packaging applies:

UK and BFPO £4.30 for one book; £6.30 for two books; £8.30 for three books.

Overseas and Eire: £4.80 for one book; £7.10 for 2 or 3 books (surface mail)

Please enclose a cheque or postal order made payable to *Bookpoint Limited*, and send to: Headline Publishing Ltd, 39 Milton Park, Abingdon, OXON OX14 4TD, UK.
Email Address: orders@bookpoint.co.uk

If you would prefer to pay by credit card, our call team would be delighted to take your order by telephone. Our direct line 01235 400 414 (lines open 9.00 am–6.00 pm Monday to Saturday 24 hour message answering service). Alternatively you can send a fax on 01235 400 454.

Name ....
Address ....
....
....

If you would prefer to pay by credit card, please complete:
Please debit my Visa/Access/Diner's Card/American Express (delete as applicable) card number:

Signature .... Expiry Date ....